About the author

On retiring, my wife and I moved from Sussex to a beautiful area in the far west of Cornwall, and 'free' time gave me the opportunity to indulge in a long-held ambition to write.

The catalyst for this novel came after exploring many themes and ideas filling pages of writing.

The novel can be read on many levels and is suitable for ages from fourteen to one-hundred-and-fourteen.

I am fortunate in having two sons (from my previous marriage) and four grandchildren. I also very much appreciate in living in a town which has a very vibrant community, is helpful and caring.

HALF LIGHT OF THE MAGIC EYE

Jack Lahmodes

HALF LIGHT OF THE MAGIC EYE

Vanguard Press

VANGUARD PAPERBACK

© Copyright 2019
Jack Lahmodes

A CIP catalogue record for this title is
available from the British Library.

ISBN 978 1 784655 12 9

*Vanguard Press is an imprint of
Pegasus Elliot MacKenzie Publishers Ltd.*
www.pegasuspublishers.com

First Published in 2019

**Vanguard Press
Sheraton House Castle Park
Cambridge England**

Printed & Bound in Great Britain

Acknowledgements

I would like to thank my wife for her support and encouragement during the years of producing this novel; also, for putting up with 'Mr. Do Not Disturb', (aka Mr. Grumpy).

I also give thanks to Pegasus publishing for their expert help and guidance in the production and editing processes.

Finally, I thank the producers of the much-enjoyed Fair Trade coffee during my two finger typing stints.

Chapter 1.

Picnic.

A droplet of water hanging from a leaf.
Planet Earth turns slowly and the droplet
aligns with the sun star,
Light reaches the moisture and scatters into
diamond colours
Which caress the retina.
The sparkling bead drops and the colours are
lost.

Rachael led them to their favourite spot. Charlie and Tom explored familiar territory, making for a large oak on the edge of the wooded clearing. The grassed area, bounded by trees, shrubs and rocky outcrops, was level and inviting. The sun, high in a cloudless sky, shone down, illuminating the area giving warmth and colour. Dark shadows were cast from overhanging ledges of the larger rocks.

Rachael and Mike began organising the picnic. They had prepared the food and drinks at home and the picnic was quickly set out. Rachael called out to Tom and Charlie, "Don't climb too high you two, food will be ready soon."

"Great," shouted Tom, who was only one branch above the ground, "I'm starving."

Charlie, now three branches higher said, "You're always hungry Mr. Piggy."

Rachael interjected, "That's enough Charlie, come on down, the picnic is ready."

They all sat down on the warm grass and began eating. Conversation dwindled as they enjoyed the spread. The sun continued to shine and peace enveloped them. Mike's feelings contradicted the prevailing aura and he said, "I don't know Rache, but the sunlight seems a bit odd, it's not like usual."

"I'm not Rache, my name is Rachael," but before she could continue her admonishment of Mike, Charlie cut in.

"Are we special then; shall we call you Lady Rachael?"

Rachael responded, "Charlie be quiet and eat your food."

"Yes miss," was Charlie's sarcastic response, but he did continue eating.

Rachael continued, "What do you mean Mike, I don't understand?"

Mike hesitated for a moment trying to crystallize his thoughts; "The colour I think, it's not the same somehow, it's yellow but not warm inside. I can't really explain it."

Rachael glanced around the picnic area and noticed the sunlight seemed to be coalescing around the food blanket; the surrounding area became dull by contrast. "Mike what's happening, the sun is on us but not beyond our area?"

Mike took a breath to reply but was interrupted by Charlie who shouted, "Look the sun's moving the light, see it's going to that big rock over there, it's like a spotlight."

"What's going on?" asked Tom through a half-eaten sandwich.

The sunlight, now iridescent, focused on a small area of rock. The spotlight became a magnet to all, especially Charlie. Rachael, Mike and Tom were transfixed and stood stock still, but Charlie interjected, "It's kind of spooky, it's like the sun is shining through a telescope." He slowly walked over to the shimmering brightness. The remaining three became hypnotized and still, as if there was an unconscious, unspoken agreement of silence as they watched him. Charlie approached the rock and stretched out his hand to touch the sun-bathed hardness of the rock and disappeared.

The three of them just stood there for a moment, not believing, not understanding. Mike shouted, "Come on Charlie, it's not funny, we have to be back after our walk in the woods by six, stop messing about, you know we're being picked up then."

Chapter 2.

Interpreter.

He looked in the mirror in front of him.
Moving slightly, he could see his back
reflected in the mirror on the opposite wall.
Turning to face the wall mirror he could see
more of his front, and behind him less of his
back.
He raised his left hand and reflected on the
right disposition in both mirrors.

They were in complete darkness, not moving or breathing, but dimly aware of each other. Slowly their eyes adjusted to the darkness, and looking around became aware of a cavern about the size of a large house. The curved walls and roof were rough and undulating, as was the floor they stood on. An area immediately in front of them showed some lightening of the gloom. Charlie said, "What's happening, how did we get here?"

Mike replied, "I don't understand, is everybody OK.?"

Rachael checked around and said, "We seem to be; where are we?"

Mike continued, "I touched the rock same as Charlie, but we were holding hands weren't we, we've all arrived here same as Charlie?"

Tom relieved the tension by shouting, "Is there anybody there, here?" his voice echoing around the dark space. Silence, a deep silence, descended in the void around them until the only audible sound was their own breathing.

"Now what do we do; is there anybody here, anybody?" Rachael's anguished voice rang out.

A soft timbered voice spoke from the rear of the cavern, "I am 'anybody'; I had to listen to you to know your language, its English I think. Is that correct?" Rachael and the others froze as if in a nightmare, not daring to move or speak. Slowly, reluctantly, they turned around to barely make out a tall, slim person (or so they assumed).

"Who are you, where are we, we don't know how we got here?" said Rachael.

"I am your Interpreter. You see the light behind you, watch and you will see the

14

blackness is surrounding it, gradually absorbing the light. There is little time, you have to decide; do you touch the light or do you wait for the light to be consumed by the darkness?"

Mike looked at Rachael, then at Tom and Charlie, and said, "I don't know. What will happen if we touch the light, that's how we got here but maybe we won't get back, I suggest we ask the, what did he call himself?"

Rachael said, "Interpreter I think, yes let's do it."

"I'll do it" said Charlie, and before anybody could challenge him he questioned the Interpreter; "What happens if we touch the light?"

The interpreter replied, "You have to choose, either you go to the light or you come with me. But hurry as the light is reducing as the blackness encroaches; look and decide."

Rachael turned to Mike and said, "I don't know what to do, what shall we do?"

Mike answered, "Neither do I, there's something spooky about the light, I'm scared to touch it. What do you Tom and Charlie think?"

Charlie butted in over Tom's voice, "Does it make any difference, either way we're stuffed. Let's trust him over there, he seems OK; what do you think Tom?"

Tom hesitated and then said, "I'm for going with him, can't explain it, but I don't want to go near the light."

The light dimmed and the blackness inexorably consumed the remaining area, becoming so dense it appeared to the onlookers like a complete void, utterly lifeless and limitless: frightening in its emptiness.

Mike said, "I'm confused, the black is scary but at the same time the light is; I don't know, it's somehow like a warning, it just doesn't feel right."

Again the four looked at each other with no enthusiasm and with a feeling of helplessness. The Interpreter did not provide encouragement or advice; he was silent. With the extinguished light and the encroaching insidious spreading blackness, all four turned to the Interpreter and communicated silently their decision to follow him.

Chapter 3.

Through the Valley.

Looking down and into the distance she was
comforted by the gentle scene.
From this distance, movement was almost
imperceptible,
Tranquillity permeated throughout.
She eschewed use of the binoculars.

The Interpreter beckoned them to follow as he turned away from the darkness. He didn't look back. They followed; keeping close to one another. The Interpreter walked at a slow and constant pace, leading the quartet along what appeared to be a tunnel exiting out of the cavern. There was just sufficient light to see their way, as they noticed they were walking along some sort of track, as the undulating rock had been worn away forming a rough pathway.

The Interpreter stopped, turned and said, "Listen to me, this is important for your safety.

We are about to enter a valley (as I think you would call it), and there may be some animals we have to pass. They are quite harmless, providing you continue walking past them quietly. Do not stare at them, there may be one or more, and do not stop walking, keep going until you are out of their sight."

"What sort of animals are they?" Charlie asked.

Tom joined in, "Yeah what are they, tigers, lions; will we be OK?"

"They are not animals you would know, they will not harm you as long as you follow the advice I have given you. Rachael and Mike, you seem to be the eldest, please ensure Charlie and Tom follow your example, as I'm sure you understand the importance of the situation."

Rachael became bemused by the Interpreter's knowledge of their names and said, "Can I ask how you know our names, and what shall we call you?"

The Interpreter merely responded, "I do not need you to tell me your names, I know them and that is sufficient. You will call me 'Interpreter' as that is what I am."

Mike accepted the apparent authority and said, "We will; Tom, Charlie keep close to us and no messing around, OK?"

"Sure, sure," said Charlie "we'll do as teacher tells us."

"Charlie that's enough now, look the Interpreter is moving, let's go. And stay together." Rachael demanded.

The Interpreter led them down some rough-cut steps. Below them they viewed a winding valley which curved away at a distance, ending the view, so they concentrated on their immediate surroundings. The valley was steep sided and covered with lush green vegetation, or rather varieties of green, ranging from vibrant translucent shrubs and grasses at the valley bottom, to blue greens to the middle areas of the slopes, and at the top lines of yellow-green large leaved and branching tree like growths. At the bottom of the valley a large flat area spread out before them and a stream of yellow water-like fluid trickled away into the distance. The valley bottom appeared marshy as light reflected off areas of yellow water interposed with vegetation. They looked at this scene feeling some form of familiarity, as they thought of water meadows, but also not recognizing any part. Mike noticed that the yellow fluid permeated throughout the valley floor, he realized there was ample light to illuminate everything before them, but then suddenly he saw movement.

"What's that?" Mike asked.

They all stopped walking.

The Interpreter said, "That's the animals, there are two of them, please respect them. Remember keep walking and do not stare."

They resumed walking along the path, which routed past both creatures. The path was dry and raised above the general marsh level. The Interpreter continued his steady pace, and the four strangers slowed as they viewed the creatures. As they drew nearer, both animals raised their heads. The Interpreter briefly nodded to them and continued walking. Charlie and Tom both looked at these strange animals who unwaveringly returned the stare of the interlopers. The animals appeared identical, each having an overall shape of a horse but with longer legs and elongated curving necks. Their skin was light yellowy ochre, smooth and hairless; there was however a deep brown upright mane and a matching twitching tail which reached the ground. As the younger boys stared the animals seemed to become agitated. They stood erect, tails swishing from side to side. Gradually, a flickering blue shimmering mosaic pattern enveloped their bodies, intensifying as the boys continued staring. The pattern pulsated, alternately fading and intensifying; random areas of bright yellow sparks flashed as if static electricity was being discharged. Their nostrils dilated and emitted showers of blue and yellow sparks in rhythm with the pulses on the body. Mike and Rachael had also become transfixed by these astonishing animals. The Interpreter continued his steady pace. Rachael suddenly understood their situation and grabbed Mike, Charlie and Tom by the arms dragging them away saying, "Come on they're getting upset, we must move on, look the Interpreter is almost out of sight." Charlie broke away and moved towards the creatures. Rachael shouted, "Charlie, come away, what are you doing?"

Charlie responded as he neared the closest animal, "I'm OK, I just want to get close that's all, don't fuss."

Charlie stopped just short of touching distance and viewed the amazing display of blues and yellows which intensified. As Mike and Rachael shouted for Charlie to 'Come away'; the nearest animal sprang sideways and quickly ran around Charlie to stop on the pathway separating him from Mike, Rachael and Tom. The other animal slowly paced onto the track in front of Charlie and raised its head, looking straight at him. The blue pulses and yellow sparks increased in frequency.

Mike shouted, "Charlie, don't move, and don't look at them. And keep quiet."

Charlie did as he was told, more through fear than instruction. The creature behind him edged forward until Charlie could feel its breath on his neck. Rachael looked for the Interpreter but he was out of sight.

The colours showed no signs of diminishing on either animal, and Mike and Rachael were at a loss to know what to do.

Tom spoke softly to Mike, "Charlie can't go around them because of the marshy ground, can he? What about trying to speak to them - I mean Charlie. Maybe he could calm them down a bit."

Mike looked at Rachael who was now close to tears. She fisted her hands, gritted her teeth and said, "Where is the Interpreter, he led us here, he should know what to do, he shouldn't disappear and leave us, we don't know what to do?" Although her voice had been muted with fear and anger the animal nearest her turned its head and stared at her intently. Rachael turned away and whispered to Mike, "Do you think it heard me, see it's looking at me, or is it just coincidence?"

As she whispered to Mike the same animal turned and faced Mike, Rachael and Tom. Tom said in his normal voice, he saw no point in further whispering, "I reckon they understand what we are saying." Mike was dubious of this idea but nevertheless hoped it would do no harm. He nodded and spoke to Charlie, "Charlie, try talking to them, Tom thinks it might help. Tell them you mean them no harm and you are sorry you have upset them." As Mike finished speaking the animal nearest to him turned around and faced Charlie again.

Charlie felt trapped and alone; his breathing was audible to all, coming in short gasps as if he were struggling for air. He said hesitantly,

"You mean I should talk to these… whatever they are."

Mike became exasperated and in a measured tone said, "Yes, what else can you do?"

Charlie took a long breath in an attempt to ease his nerves and spoke to the animal in front of him, "I'm sorry if I upset you, honestly I didn't mean any harm."

Mike noticed a slight diminution of colour intensity and sparks on the one facing Charlie, but not on the one behind him. Mike encouraged by the slight reaction said, "I think it's working Charlie. Try turning around slowly, very slowly, and speaking to the other one."

Charlie did as he was told, concentrating on keeping his movements as controlled and steady as possible. He now faced the creature standing between himself and the others. Summoning a breath of confidence, he spoke directly at the animal but avoided looking into its eyes, "Please, I didn't mean any harm, I just wanted to see you properly; will you let me go?"

The animal's sparking coloured envelope increased until its body shape became a mist of swirling shapes, colours and flashes of light. Charlie was transfixed by the display, unable to move or cry out with alarm. Rachael began to shout a warning when the animal raised its head high and opened its mouth and expelled a shower of sparks, some of which fell on Charlie.

Charlie jumped and yelled, "Hey, stop it, I don't like it."

Rachael became alarmed but Mike restrained her from interceding.

Tom stepped forward and said, "Hold on Charlie, I think that was a warning, look he's calming down."

As Tom finished speaking, both animals stepped off the track and into the marsh, each watching the youngsters with an intensity which Mike interpreted as a further warning. He spoke firmly, "Right, all of us must now go, I think we've been allowed to carry on our way. Charlie give your thanks and be quick to follow us."

On this occasion Charlie obeyed without question, said his thanks to each animal and quickly joined the others. Without looking back, they hurried on to search for the Interpreter.

They eventually joined up with the Interpreter who was sitting on a grass mound apparently waiting for them.

Mike said, "What would have happened if we hadn't spoken to them, do you know what happened?"

"You did and you made the best choice, I can therefore lead you on to the next part of your journey."

Chapter 4.

Right Hookers.

Certainty was the guiding light,
The true path would lead to the 'Way', the
only way.
Momentum built, the rhythm feeling good,
progress moved on inexorably.
The barrier across the 'Way' was strong and
built with conviction.

Leaving the valley and following the Interpreter the group entered a plateau; everywhere was level and devoid of vegetation. They could dimly make out some form of ramparts or buildings in the far distance. The Interpreter pointed towards them and said, "Follow me." As they trudged across the plain a thick orangey brown dust swirled around their feet, spreading upwards till they breathed in an acrid dry smoke-like fume. Coughing, and with eyes watering, they looked to the Interpreter for reassurance. He said, "Try not to breathe in too deeply, as long as we reach the city over there in good time we will be safe."

Mike asked, "Why; is this stuff poisonous?"

"Only if you take in too much, let's hurry, we need to get there before dark."

The Interpreter quickened his pace and the others followed. Tom brought up the rear puffing and complaining.

"Come on porky you can do it, look it's only another twenty miles!" said Charlie.

Rachael intervened, "Never mind him Tom, if you need a hand just shout."

Tom retorted, "No thanks, I can manage, no worries."

As they approached the city they could make out massive walls of stone, they assumed it was stone, surmounted by overhanging ramparts some thirty metres above ground level. Piercing the wall in front of them was a doorway three metres high and two metres wide, with the opening supported by a huge stone lintel. Inset in the opening was a door, which was massive, forbidding and overpowering. It was absolutely smooth, black and impenetrable. No hinges were visible and there was one small odd shaped aperture at low level, possibly for a key.

The Interpreter walked over to the door, took something out of his pocket, the others could not see what it was, and slid it into the opening, turning it twice and returning it to his pocket. He stepped back and waited. Slowly the door swung inwards, making no sound, coming to a halt at right angles to the walling. The door edge showed about thirty centimetres thickness, and the same black smoothness as the face. The Interpreter walked through the opening and signalled the others to follow. The door swung silently shut behind them.

They crossed a level area devoid of any life; the ground being barren and dark, but without the previous obnoxious dust. They were confronted by more massive ramparts, similar to the outer boundary walling. Approaching an opening in the wall at ground level, they were confronted by a line of 'Persons', all of them exactly the same distance apart from one another, and all looking in the same direction. The sentinels appeared to be men of sorts, dressed in dark brown plain uniforms, with shoes matching the colour of the outer entry door.

Rachael was the first to notice that all the men, there were no women judging by appearances, were looking across their right shoulders, not moving their heads at all. Their eyes were also fixed and centred on the doorway. Rachael said quietly to Mike, "Don't make it obvious, but they are all looking the same way and not moving at all."

The others agreed and looked at the Interpreter. He said, "That's better, well done. Now don't spoil it, follow me."

"He always speaks in riddles, doesn't he?" said Charlie.

Mike replied, "Yes he does, I guess it's up to us to figure it out."

Tom joked, "Like a TV Quiz show you mean?"

"Not exactly Tom," Mike said smiling to himself.

The Interpreter interrupted them: "Now listen, I have to see some 'Persons', I think you would call them 'People', and I will arrange for us to pass through the city tomorrow. Please find a place to rest and I will return soon."

Tom piped up, "Can you bring us some food, I'm starving?"

"Yes of course, and I hope you like it as it will be all we can have. I will return soon."

The four sat down against some stone walling. Mike said, "At least that disgusting dust isn't in here, I wonder what it was; anyway we need to have a chat, I for one haven't the faintest idea where we are or what's happening. Are we dreaming, surely, we can't all be dreaming the same dream? Who or what is the Interpreter? Yes, he seems OK, but we don't know anything about him?"

"I know, but we're here; pinch me if you like but I bet you it will hurt," said Rachael.

"I'll do it" said Charlie, "Give me your arm."

"This is serious Charlie; we've got to decide what to do."

Charlie responded, "Why don't we go back the way we came, we know the way and we can get past those animals, and then chance it getting back through that rock?"

Tom joined in, "I'm not keen, the door in the boundary wall is shut and we don't know if we can get through the rock even if we did get there."

Charlie thought for a moment, and then said, "Well I'm not waiting here forever. I suggest we sit here for a while and if there's no sign of him we give it a go trying to get back." He continued immediately not wanting any contradiction, "All agreed."

Rachael didn't; "No Charlie, we stay together and wait. We seem safe enough here and he said he would return."

Charlie retorted, "Like he did with those crazy animals."

Mike cut in, "That's enough Charlie, we must wait for his return, he may be our only protection."

After an interminable time, or so it seemed to Charlie, he got to his feet and stated, "Well I'm fed up with all this hanging about. I'm going back, anyone coming?"

"Charlie wait, you can't go on your own, give it a bit longer," said Rachael.

Charlie moved away, retracing his steps and said, "I've waited long enough; I'm going to give it a try."

Rachael looked at Mike who said, "I can't physically stop him, who knows what might happen if we caused a ruckus here. I'll have to go with him and if it looks like we can get out

I'll come back for you both. If not then we'll both come back."

Rachel and Mike both stood up and Rachael tried once more to keep them all together, "Do you have to, I don't like us being split up?"

Mike nodded and made the decision, "You and Tom stay here in case the Interpreter returns. You can explain where we've gone and let's hope he will wait."

Rachael and Tom watched Mike and Charlie walk away, heading in the direction of the opening in the rampart walling they had previously passed through. Approaching the opening they noticed a line of the strange right-looking people to one side, as if guarding the opening but not blocking the way through. As they approached the opening the line of 'People' moved to their right passing across the opening and curving around to stop, forming an arc behind the two puzzled onlookers.

"Looks like they're giving us the all clear, what do you reckon Mike?" said Charlie.

Mike agreed and suggested they move cautiously forward. As they passed through the portal they looked back to see the 'People' move to complete the circle and return to their original position.

"Well, that was easy," said Charlie, "Let's hope the next bit is just as simple; let's get a move on."

Mike increased his pace to keep up with Charlie. He remembered the Interpreter had used some key device to open the door from the outside and hoped this would not be needed to open it from the inside, otherwise they were stuck. "Charlie, if we can open that massive great door, don't go through. We'll return and collect Rach and Tom," he said.

"Don't let Rachael hear you call her that or you will be in deep trouble," Mike replied, "We're in enough trouble now, so let's concentrate on that."

They could now make out the huge door which seemed even more forbidding with its dominating size and blackness, partially wreathed in rising dust, appearing as if it were breathing as the dust rose and subsided.

Mike stopped and grasped Charlie's arm, "Hold on Charlie, look there's more of those whatever they are, but they are all across the door, looks like they are on guard. What do you think?"

Charlie thought for a moment and said, "They are the same as the others, they're all looking one way, to their right, and they don't move their heads. So why don't we go over to the end of the line, the end they are not looking at, and see if we can get to the door?"

"OK, but let's take it slow and careful, and see what happens," said Mike.

They edged their way over to the end of the line of 'People' so they were facing away from them. Mike whispered, "So far, so good. Easy now we are nearly there."

As they approached the key hole aperture and attempted to push against the door bulk, one of the 'People' moved away from the would-be escapees to form the now familiar circular movement, but this time forming a complete semi-circle, with both extremities coming to a stop against the door. Mike and Charlie were now trapped and the door made no sign of moving, despite their frantic pushing and shouldering against the solid blackness.

Realising the door might only open inwards, Mike took stock of the situation as Charlie shouldered against the door without effect. "Charlie, maybe the door only opens in, there's nothing to get hold of and we haven't the key thing. Let's think this through; there must be a way to escape," said Mike.

Charlie just shrugged with open arms and looked at Mike.

Mike spoke as if he had had a sudden idea, "You remember when you were trapped by those animals? Tom had the idea of talking to them. Why don't we try talking to these, whatever they are, 'People'?"

Charlie unenthusiastically agreed and said, "Can't do any harm, I suppose."

"Let's hope not," said Mike, and he turned to inspect their captors in detail. He failed to make out any distinguishing mark of seniority, any special uniform or badge denoting rank. He spoke quietly to Charlie, "Here goes, watch for any reactions."

"Wait. Why don't we rush at them and barge our way through? They seem incapable of movement other than going around in circles, and we could duck low and I bet they wouldn't be quick enough to stop us or catch us," said Charlie.

Mike disagreed, "No Charlie, we mustn't be aggressive, it's not our place and we don't know how they would react. No, let's try talking and see what transpires." Mike took a small pace forwards and spoke to the assembly, "I don't know if you can understand what I am saying but we want to go back to our friends and wait for the Interpreter, will you let us pass?"

The assembly had shown no signs of comprehension, no movement or reaction at all until Mike had mentioned the Interpreter. At this word the semi-circle began to move to their right, slowly walking behind Mike and Charlie until they stopped, now forming an arc across the doorway as if emphasizing the door would not be opened. The space in front of Mike and Charlie was clear. Looking at each other they began walking, with Mike restraining Charlie's impulse to run.

Mike turned to Charlie and said, "We got out of that Charlie, but it seems clear we can't go back through that doorway, so let's find Rachael and Tom. Hope we haven't missed the Interpreter."

Charlie agreed and kept pace with Mike as they tried not to hurry, but they were especially eager to be re-united with the others.

They had a free pass through the portal and soon saw Rachael and Tom in the distance. Waving, they joined the others, who both had relieved smiles.

Rachael spoke first; "How did you get on, are you both OK?"

Mike dismissed her anxiety with: "We're fine; no way out through that black door though, looks like we wait. I take it the Interpreter hasn't been back?"

Before Rachael or Tom could reply, the Interpreter appeared through an opening in the stone walling and said, "You are all here in spite of Charlie's impetuousness, good, we can proceed, follow me?"

Charlie attempted to protest but Mike interjected, "Charlie, be quiet." He turned to Rachael and confided his thoughts; "I reckon he knows exactly what's going on all the time. I'll explain about Charlie later." Turning to the others he said, "Right, we will follow the Interpreter and no wandering off or mucking about."

For once Charlie didn't resort to sarcasm, he merely said, "OK at least the Interpreter seems to know his way around and we're safe so far."

The Interpreter then said, "Charlie, there is hope for you yet."

Tom wavered, and said, "I know Charlie but I'm not really sure, I want to go home and see mum and dad."

Rachael joined in, "Yes we all do but we must think carefully. I suggest when the time is right we insist he answers our questions. What do you think?"

"I agree" said Mike.

"Come on we must keep together and work this out, we must," said Rachael.

The Interpreter raised his hand and said, "I cannot answer your questions. We have to go into the city as it is not safe to stay outside tonight."

"Why not?" asked Rachael.

The Interpreter insisted, "Please follow me and I will show you when we are inside."

They all passed through a doorway. The 'Persons' stared at them as they walked past but did not move their heads. Inside the group examined the buildings and failed to notice any significant variation in design from the outer area, apart from a few higher buildings. One building did stand out as it was considerably taller and wider than the rest, and the group appeared to be heading towards it. The interpreter approached what was possibly a sentry at the main entrance signified by some form of railings across an opening. He stopped alongside the sentry and held up the item he had used on the outer door. He had to hold it in such a position so the sentry looking across his right shoulder, as the other 'People' had done, could clearly see the entry talisman. The sentry turned to his right and inserted his own key into the railings which then slid to one side. The sentry moved on in a circular path returning to his original position.

Charlie began to say, "Why did he…"

Then, all of a sudden, the Interpreter stopped him and said, "Charlie you learn but slowly. Now come, the railings will shut."

They all walked past the railings which silently closed behind them. The room they entered was large and imposing by its austerity. The walls were plain and yellowish brown; the ceiling high above them similarly coloured, but with hanging shapes which could be some form of lighting. The floor was a mixture of cream with light brown to dark brown, in which a black and white motif pattern occupied the centre. It was about two metres in diameter and consisted of a clockwise spiral design emanating from the centre. Arranged around part of the spiral was an arc of seated 'Persons', all with heads aligned to the right and so positioned to view the strangers as they entered.

One of the seated 'Persons' said, "Stop there. Interpreter you have been authorized to conduct your friends through the city but we have a crisis. The One Sighted Army have broken into our stores and stolen some of our special binoculars. They are no good to them but we use them in battle so you see the importance of this situation?"

The Interpreter then spoke, "My friends are grateful for your permission and they ask why you need to go to war and with whom?"

Rachael looked at Mike and whispered, "I was going to ask that, how did he know?"

"Beats me, I was going too as well."

The spokesman said, "The OSA is our enemy. We have built the outer walls as a defence and cleared the ground beyond the walls. We have also seeded the ground with a poison which, if inhaled for a long period, causes drowsiness and death. Thus, we have good defences but still they manage to break in from time to time."

His voice changed and he spoke in a commanding manner. "Now attention all of you, you must pass through our city quickly or you will have to remain here until we have defeated them, do you understand?"

The Interpreter gave his thanks and urged the four to follow him without delay. Charlie attempted to ask more questions but was ignored by the Interpreter who walked unusually briskly across the room to an open door.

Tom asked, "What about the food you promised?"

Without turning, the Interpreter said, "Time enough for eating when we are safe. No more talking, just walk and cause no delay."

Charlie said to Tom, "He's getting a bit stroppy isn't he, we'd better get going I suppose?"

"Charlie!" Rachael scolded, "No talking he said, now come on and be quiet."

"OK, OK, mum's the word."

They exited the room and entered a long corridor with rooms opening off both sides.

The Interpreter warned; "Remember, no talking."

As they walked along this 'tunnel' they saw more people with heads twisted to their right shoulder and unbelieving saw them traverse from area to area always in a circular route; the buildings seemed to be designed to accommodate this strange behaviour. Continuing through, they eventually came to a large door set in heavy stonework. The Interpreter used his talisman again, this time opening the door himself which swung silently to reveal a similar door about three metres ahead. The masonry surrounding this door was even heavier than the first, and Mike guessed it was set within the outer boundary wall. A stone spiral flight of steps adjacent to the gateway led up to the ramparts. Three 'People' stood sideways at the top, using their special binoculars to view areas beyond the wall. One turned, acknowledging the Interpreter's brief nod. Holding up his hand to halt the would-be exiters he said, "You wait until the all clear."

"Does that mean we can eat now?" said Tom.

"I thought we weren't supposed to be talking," said Charlie.

Rachael, exasperated, said, "Charlie don't be cheeky, stop it."

The rampart 'Person' signalled the Interpreter to proceed. The Interpreter gave thanks and opened the door in the usual way. Outside the enclosure it was still dark and it took some time for them to adjust to the low level of light. The Interpreter then informed them; "We will now walk over to the woods over there, it will conceal us, should there be fighting in this area: follow closely." He then added, "Tom, we can eat when we get there."

"Great," said Tom, "I can't wait, I'm starving."

In the fading light the woods revealed an indistinct outline in the far distance, and they strode towards this haven, following closely behind the Interpreter. As they approached the woods they could dimly make out trunks which reached upwards disappearing in the gloom. Entry into the woods seemed somewhat similar to the cavern in which they had commenced their journey. They hesitated and were encouraged by the Interpreter to follow closely. They joined up and entered the darkness. As they slowly penetrated deeper into the wood they became aware of a gentle illumination of the surrounding area. They could clearly see tree trunks around them. All were yellow and without branches, apart from the top ten metres. The branches arched out, overhanging and intermingling with branches of adjoining trees. Leafy protuberances spread along the branches in a ferny structure. Mike looked up and wondered why it was light in the woods; he could see clearly for some distance and then realized the light was emanating from the trunks, providing sufficient illumination to ease navigation. The area beneath the canopy was strangely shadow-less.

The Interpreter, whilst removing packages from within his tunic said, "Sit down here and we can eat."

They all sat down and he handed packages to Mike for distribution. Tom unwrapped his food and began munching. He looked up and said to the Interpreter, "Tastes good, what is it?"

"It's not something you would know, if you like it, it's good."

Rachael broke in, "How do we know it's not bad for us, we don't know what it is, it has a peculiar smell?"

Charlie joined in, "I'm not eating any old thing; surely you can give us some idea?"

"If you don't want it, I'll have it," said Tom.

The Interpreter responded firmly, "You will be hungry if you don't eat, and sometimes you have to place trust; use your judgement."

"Here we go again" said Charlie, "more riddles and no answers. Oh well here goes."

Eventually they ate their meal. All agreed, although somewhat strange tasting, or rather an unusual unknown taste, the food was good and satisfying.

The Interpreter stood up and said, "Time to move on, we have a long way to go."

Charlie whispered to Tom, "He could get on my nerves, he's always talking in riddles, he could be the Joker for all we know!"

"Then let's hope Batman's around!" Tom said, and smiled feeling the satisfaction of a full stomach.

"Come," instructed the Interpreter as he moved through the trees away from the city.

Chapter 5.

Smelly.

He loved stroking the warm coat,
The feeling was mutual and reciprocated.
An affinity developed.

They travelled through the woods following the Interpreter. The tree trunk light, pale yellow and evenly spread, created a feeling of contentment and they soon became relaxed and confident. The light from the tree trunks seemed to be triggered by their presence, fading behind them and lighting up as they progressed through the woods. As they reached the edge of the woods the light faded and once more they stumbled through greyness, closely following the Interpreter. Reluctant to step into daylight, Tom said, "What's the time?"

"Don't know, my watch has stopped," said Charlie.

The Interpreter interjected, "Time is unimportant here, there is no sun as you know it."

"We get the message," said Charlie.

"I don't think you do Charlie," replied the Interpreter, and the woodland spell vanished; they looked outwards away from the trees.

In front of them lay an open rock-strewn plateau stretching to the horizon. Various sized rocks littered the area, some sharp and angular, others smooth and rounded. They varied in colour from grey sharp ones, to creamy yellow rounded ones. There appeared to be no clear way through, and any indication of a pathway could not be discerned. The children hesitated at the edge and looked into the far distance. Indistinct mauve undulations terminated the plateau and the Interpreter paced out in his usual steady rhythm heading away from them.

"Where's he off to now?" said Charlie, speaking to no one in particular.

"Who cares" said Tom, "as long as we get something to eat and drink, I'm thirsty."

"Tom you are a dustbin with no bottom" joked Charlie.

"Never mind all that you two, we'd better follow him, we can't stay here," ordered Mike.

"Yes let's go, it looks a bit tricky with all those rocks to navigate," agreed Rachael.

They followed the Interpreter and found the going much harder than they had anticipated. Each picked their own route around the sharp and irregular stony outcrops and loose boulders. Progress was slow and the Interpreter appeared to be diminishing in size.

"Keep together everyone in case we lose him," said Rachael.

Eventually the rocks reduced in quantity and size. This enabled them to speed up and they hastened to catch up with their leader.

The mauve shapes proved to be green foliated trees, and the Interpreter sat in their shade, resting. The followers arrived and sat down a little distance from him to cool off.

"I'm so hot," said Tom, "what I wouldn't give for a drink."

The Interpreter got up, and holding a small cylindrical shaped container, removed the lid, leant to his side and dipped it into a stream of clear water. Lifting it to his mouth he drank until it was empty.

"Hey" yelled Tom, "I didn't know there was any water there, I'm going to get some."

"Hold on Tom," said Mike, "how do we know it's safe for us, we'd better ask him first?"

"He drank it, so why can't we?" questioned Tom.

"He's not like us is he; better ask first to make sure," Mike insisted.

"OK, OK, but let's get on with it," Grumbled Tom.

Rachael stood up, went over to the Interpreter and said: "Is it alright for us to drink the water?" As she spoke she looked at the hitherto unseen stream. The stream followed a sinuous route and was absolutely clear; she could see no debris, plants, fish or other living creatures, only the stony bottom, each stone being perfectly visible. The stones were varying shades of white and the surface of the liquid rippled slightly reflecting the light as a shimmering haze. Rachael realized she was becoming mesmerized by the subtle light waves.

The Interpreter broke her trance; "Yes you can all drink from the stream and I would like to know what you think of the taste."

Rachael signalled to all to come and drink. They cupped their hands and drank. The Interpreter didn't have to ask the question again, as one by one they exclaimed the water to be the 'most delicious and satisfying taste they had ever experienced.' They felt invigorated and sat down again feeling strangely at peace.

The reverie was shattered by Tom's exclamation: "What is that smell?"

"What smell Tom, hold on, yes, I've got it now, it's disgusting?" said Charlie.

"Yes, I can smell it too," said Mike.

"So can I," agreed Rachael, "what on earth is it?"

The Interpreter said in a monotone: "You are not on earth now, so put aside your judgements."

Tom saw the movement first; "Look, over there, by that rock, the larger one; I'm sure I saw something move."

"You know Tom I reckon that smell reminds me of that food we ate, do you remember, smelt funny but tasted not bad?" said Charlie.

"You're right Charlie" said Mike, "it's the same, let's see if we can spot the cause; all eyes on Tom's rock but spread out so we get a wider view."

The four walked slowly away from each other, gradually surrounding the rock but at a distance. Having completed the circle, step by step they eased towards their quarry. Rachael thought they should perhaps check with the Interpreter, she looked across to him but he showed no interest in them. Although she took this to be a positive sign she was perplexed at his lack of interest.

"I can see it!" exclaimed Tom, "it's hiding at the bottom of the rock, in the shade, I saw it move."

"What is it?" shouted Charlie.

"Quiet Charlie, it crouched down when you yelled" Mike warned, "Don't get close, we don't know if it's safe."

They all looked to the Interpreter who continued to ignore them.

"Now what do we do?" asked Tom.

The creature, if that was what it was, continued crouching by the rock. They gathered together and viewed it, but didn't want to frighten it away. They saw a hedgehog sized 'animal', greyish brown with an irregular bedraggled covering of fur; the hairs of which were oriented front to back. The face, as far as they could see, was round with a tapering dark brown nose which seemed to be tasting the air. It had two intense black eyes, which constantly flickered in all directions.

They approached very slowly, hoping the creature would move a little and show its full extent.

"I think we should leave it alone and not disturb it; it's not doing us any harm," said Rachael.

"Other than the pong!" said Charlie.

"Yes, alright," said Mike, "let's leave it and see what the Interpreter is up to."

They re-joined the Interpreter who got to his feet and said, "All safe then?"

Without waiting for a reply he moved off downstream along a path of finely broken rock, which was white and crunchy underfoot. The path was bordered on one side by the stream and the other side by low growing, green 'shrubs' and trees. Light filtered through the foliage and reflected off the stream and path. The inevitable question was asked, this time by Mike: "Where are we going?"

To their amazement they received a clear answer.

"I thought you might be interested in a place called 'Electric City'," said the Interpreter.

Chapter 6.

Electric City.

Energy pulsed along the arteries
spreading vein to vein,
ever flowing and permeating every channel,
surging and ebbing, unaware of itself
or its involvement in hurt.

Charlie and Tom were excited by the Interpreter's response and chatted in anticipation. They thought they had better not question him further, fearing that they would receive a typical enigmatic response. Mike and Rachael followed the others along the pathway.

"Mike, what are we doing; we're traipsing after the Interpreter to all sorts of places not knowing where we are, what's happening or what's to become of us?" said Rachael.

"I know" said Mike, "but we haven't come to any harm yet, and anyway what choice do we have?"

Their misgivings were interrupted by Charlie and Tom, and Charlie shouting "Come on, you dawdlers, this should be good."

The Interpreter stopped and turned to face them and said, "Do you like Robots?"

"You bet" said Tom.

"What sort of robots?" asked Charlie.

"Soon you will see," said the Interpreter.

He continued along the path, followed more closely than usual by Tom and Charlie; Mike and Rachael hesitated and then reluctantly joined them.

The vegetation gradually diminished and the stony path became a uniform black with edges both sides delineated by perfectly straight and continuous board-like material, showing no joints or evidence of its make-up. The stream veered away from the path to disappear amongst vegetation in the distance.

Tom and Charlie exclaimed: "Look at that, that's incredible!"

In the near distance stood a vast monument; squat, square, forbidding, save for festoons of dazzling lights on all surfaces. The lights glowed with varying intensities, changing subtly from yellows to reds, then to greens to blues and all combinations in between so that the viewers only slowly realized as they drew nearer, that the massed effects transposed as three-dimensional animations of 'creatures', 'people', 'plant life' or anything the imagination allowed.

"Wow," Charlie exhaled, "that's something special, do you get it, you lot?"

"We do and yes it's pretty spectacular" said Mike.

"Look, there's more things coming, it changes all the time," said Charlie.

Rachael looked around and could not see the Interpreter. "Mike, did you see where the Interpreter went, I can't see him?"

"No, I didn't, he can't be far, Tom, Charlie did you see where he went?"

Both boys shook their heads and continued watching the display. Rachael pointed to a large opening in the wall. It appeared more like a portal than doorway, but it was the only visible way into the complex. As they passed through the opening Charlie stopped, looked around and said: "There's that smell again, don't say it's following us."

The others tested the air and agreed; yes there was no mistaking that pungent odour.

"Don't worry it won't follow us in here, come on let's go we have to find the Interpreter," said Mike.

"What if 'Smelly' does follow us, what do we do?" queried Tom.

"Never mind" Rachael urged, "we must move on."

And they did, in some haste, as they searched for their leader. Their urgency became mitigated as they felt a wobbly sensation as they moved forward.

"This path, or whatever it is, seems to move slightly every time we move, can you feel it?" said Mike.

"Yes, I wondered why I felt as if I was going to lose my balance. Charlie, Tom, how are you doing?" replied Rachael.

"I thought the path was loose or something, but you're right, it does seem to move when we move," said Charlie.

"Look, if you step off the edge there's no movement, it's just ground," said Tom.

"We'll just have to be careful," said Mike.

Rachael looked up and took stock of the area confronting them. The 'People', who busily hurried in all directions, walked on the pathways without any problems.

"Look over there," shouted Mike, as he pointed towards the disappearing shape of the Interpreter between many colourful and dazzling 'shop' fronts.

They all found it difficult to hurry after the Interpreter on the moving pathway. The shops, or what appeared to be shops, demanded their attention. They consisted of mostly single storey units, all with brilliant lighting displays with ever changing colours. The kaleidoscopic colours were accompanied by subtle harmonic sounds synchronizing with the changing lights. All four became apprehensive as they quickly realized a great many 'People' thronged the entire area, entering and leaving the shops at regular intervals. The 'People' were generally tall, relative to themselves, and slim. Others who were less numerous, appeared shorter and stockier. Both types had small ears laid flat against their heads and vestiges of a nose with a single nostril. They had small mouths. The children were struck by the odd appearance of the 'People' and were fascinated by their eyes. These were intense, black and roved side to side and up and down in a rhythmic pattern. Not once did the children observe them look directly at them.

Most wore all-in-one clothes from neck to ankles of various shades. The tall ones entered a certain type of shop, which appeared to the children as some sort of café, and sat down to swallow coloured drinks through tubes. They conversed with their immediate neighbours, some remaining in their seats, others leaving at frequent intervals.

Mike turned to Rachael and said: "Have you noticed that nobody takes any notice of us, it's like we're invisible?"

"Yes" agreed Rachael, "it looks as though we don't exist; I think we're pretty safe."

The two gathered up Charlie and Tom and steered them through alleyways between low profiled houses away from the shops, urging them to keep together and to look out for the Interpreter. After a fruitless search they agreed to stop and take a rest.

"We seem to be getting nowhere. Anyone got any suggestions?" said Mike.

"Let's face it we're lost and without the Interpreter we don't know what to do or where to go," replied Rachael.

"I don't like this place, it gives me the jitters, can't say why, it just does," said Tom.

Charlie put his arm on Tom's shoulder and quietly said, "Its OK Tom, we're all together, and his nibs will turn up eventually, we'll be OK."

Mike was encouraged by Charlie's faith in the Interpreter appearing at some stage. Nevertheless, they all became silent and wished they were home and safe. Nobody spoke as the mood of despair permeated through them.

Charlie shook his head and said, "I've had enough of this, I'm not giving up, come on let's have another go at finding what's his name. Who's coming?"

They continued their search but were distracted by the bright lights and sounds of the shops, eventually arriving at an open area they had not previously explored. The area was circular and clear of obstructions, and its circumference was delineated by a series of bunkers. Some were one and a half metres high, others much lower. The fronts had various shapes and protuberances of differing colours. The group stopped to consider a plan of action. Again, the feeling of being alone and lost and the empty space somehow exacerbated their feelings. Their guide and leader was nowhere to be seen.

Before they could shake themselves out of their introspection, an unearthly sound impinged on their consciousness and they all looked up at the sky. A flying machine appeared overhead and cast a dark shadow over the area. The children stood transfixed, looking up to the underside of a large cylindrical grey shape with protuberances at each end, and two more midway along each side. Mike was the first to realize this machine was slowly descending, preparing to settle on the ground, and shouted, "Look out it's coming down, run!"

All four scurried over to the entry point of the area and turned to watch. The craft noisily extended six leg supports and grumbled and creaked to rest on the solid ground. As they watched and waited for something to happen, groups of the stocky 'People' entered the arena and began opening the fronts of the bunkers from which they withdrew series of coloured hoses. With coordinated actions each team manoeuvred the hoses over to the craft and connected them to similarly coloured sockets. As one, they returned to their respective bunkers to operate switches. A low-level hissing sound emanated from the hoses which oscillated snake like on the ground to rear up and feed the grey inanimate beast with life giving energy. A series of dull clunks sounded from within the bunkers; the hissing noise subsided and the 'People' disconnected the hoses from the machine. They walked to the bunkers and pressed a switch, which resulted in the snakes slowly returning to their homes. Bunker doors shut silently and the 'People' trooped out of the arena totally ignoring the children.

"Hey, that was impressive; do you reckon that thing is going to take off?" said Charlie.

"Let's wait and see, should be pretty spectacular," said Tom.

"We can't stay here wasting time; we must find the Interpreter as we don't know where to go or anything," responded Rachael.

"Oh come on, five minutes won't hurt" said Charlie.

"I think Rachael's right Charlie", said Mike, "We're lost and don't know anything about this place. We must decide what we're going to do."

Heads down, Charlie and Tom mumbled agreement and followed Rachael and Mike to the entrance position. Mike looked at Rachael shrugging his shoulders and hesitating briefly, led them back amongst the shops and cafés.

They became aware the dazzling colours they had previously admired had changed, causing them to slow down to investigate. These were now muted and slow in changing from one hue to another.

Mike became impatient, "Come on you two we will never find him at this rate."

"OK, OK we're coming, we're coming; I wanted to explore a bit, but I suppose we have to follow," said Charlie. Turning to Tom he said, "Come on Tom let's see who can see our man first" and he walked briskly ahead beckoning Tom to follow.

"Keep together," urged Mike, "I thought you were going to follow, Charlie".

They moved with purpose and continued along the alleyways. Mike saw at a distance a green glow apparently suspended in air. "Look, let's head for that light and then see what we should do."

"What light?" queried Charlie.

"Up in the air, can you all see it, the green one, we'll go there."

They agreed and made for the beacon. Arriving they gathered together and took stock of their situation.

"What do we do now?" Tom questioned.

"Well, I reckon we should split up, have a look around to find the Interpreter, but in any case, we'll all meet back here in say fifteen minutes," said Mike.

They checked their watches and found them not to be working. "Mine's not going" said Tom.

"What, your Mickey Mouse job, I'm not surprised," Charlie jibed. He confidently checked his own watch and exclaimed: "hang on, mine's not going either."

"Mine neither, how's yours Rach, sorry, Rachael?" said Mike.

"No mine has stopped, what's going on?"

"Never mind" said Mike, "we can guess fifteen minutes, but in any case, we must all keep the green light in sight, so we can get back here."

Before they could respond a voice, they recognized said, "Follow me and make sure you don't wander."

"Where did he spring from?" asked Tom.

"Never mind Tom, thank goodness he's here now, come on, he's moving away," said Rachael.

The Interpreter walked at his usual pace under the green light and out of the complex. They looked back to see nothing but black, blank walling with no hint of the light and colours within, even the green light was invisible.

"Hang on a minute" said Charlie, addressing himself to the Interpreter, "You said we would see some robots, didn't you?"

"Charlie don't be rude" admonished Rachael.

The Interpreter turned to Charlie and said in a monotone, "Did you not see them?" and with that he turned and continued his journey.

Chapter 7.

New Vision.

As they looked beyond
and did see,
They persevered and acquired some
tranquillity.

They followed the Interpreter along a straight pathway covered with stone slabs of equal size and close-fitting joints. "Off we go again" said Charlie.

"I'm hungry and I can still smell 'Smelly'," said Tom.

"So can I and I'm hungry as well," replied Mike.

"Don't say you are becoming like Tom," said Charlie, "not two of you; where is that pong coming from, it must be following us or there are lots of them?"

The Interpreter stopped, turned and said to Charlie, "Best to make friends with, what do you call him, 'Smelly', as he will need your protection later."

"How do I do that, I can't see him and in any case I'm not sure I want to be friends unless I can find a peg?"

The Interpreter fixed his eyes on Charlie's and said, "Have you thought of being kind?" He turned and recommenced walking.

"Come on Charlie, we'll help you, it can't be dangerous or the Interpreter wouldn't encourage us, would he?" said Rachael.

"I suppose not but where is it?" Charlie said, looking around and seeing no sign of the creature; he continued, "Here 'Smelly', good boy, we won't hurt you."

To their amazement 'Smelly' slowly crept into view from behind a low mound. He stopped and looked at them, nose quivering and eyes searching everywhere.

"What happens now?" said Tom.

"Let's try getting nearer to him" said Mike, "but slowly we don't want to scare him off."

As they eased their way towards him 'Smelly' backed away maintaining the exact same distance from them.

"Stop," said Rachael, "this is no good, let's walk away and see if he follows." And he did.

If they stopped, he stopped, always keeping the same distance away.

"OK," said Mike, "we'll catch up with the Interpreter and see if he follows. Keep an eye on him to make sure."

"Yes Sir" said Charlie, but they ignored him.

Hurrying on Tom reported regularly that 'Smelly' was close by.

Reaching the Interpreter, who walked his regular stride, they enquired as to what they should do to get closer to 'Smelly'. He replied by saying, "Trust is shared, and it's not one way. Why should he trust you?"

"This bloke gives me a headache," grumbled Charlie.

"Charlie! I've told you before, do not be rude," Rachael became angry and Mike held up a conciliatory hand.

"Calm down everybody, we're all stressed out but it makes sense."

"Not to me," Charlie sulked.

Mike continued, "As the Interpreter said, why should 'Smelly' trust us? We must somehow find a way of gaining his confidence in us."

"Yes but how?" asked Tom.

"Let's carry on and see what happens, I reckon he will follow now and we can decide as we go along."

"Brilliant," said Charlie sarcastically.

"Lead on o' great leaders," said Tom, "Charlie ease up, I quite like having 'Smelly' around, I reckon I would miss him now."

"You can have him and the pong."

"Stop sulking Charlie" Rachael admonished, "and hurry we are losing sight of the Interpreter."

They gained on the Interpreter and Mike turned to Rachael and asked, "I know we're hungry but I wonder what 'Smelly' eats?"

The Interpreter stopped, turned his head towards the children and said, "We will all eat soon, 'Smelly' will be fine for now, we must move on."

They walked on and Rachael noticed a dark mass in the distance. The outline stood sharp and angular against a shimmering ink blue-grey sky. To one side the darkness gave way to a warm yellow red glow reminding Rachael of the open fire at home. She became quiet and felt empty and alone.

"You OK?" said Mike.

"Yes I'll be fine, come on; I think we're heading towards that light over there."

"Sure" said Mike and he put his arm around her and said, "Somehow I feel everything is going to be alright."

"Of course," said Rachael.

They approached the glow which emanated from an entranceway and felt drawn in with a feeling of comfort and security. The Interpreter led them through the opening into a huge cavern. They crossed a flat area, over to a high bank. The bank reached up to an angular and facetted ceiling five metres above them. The ceiling reflected the warm glow and illuminated the surrounding walls. Set into the bank side were serried rows of what appeared to be flat metal plates, each about twenty centimetres long by fifteen wide. The plates were engraved in blue hieroglyphics.

"What's all those funny squiggles mean and what's in the boxes?" asked Tom.

"They are boxes, Tom, you are correct; the 'squiggles' identify the contents, and I can understand them."

"What's in them?" said Charlie who had become interested and went up to them.

"Later" said the Interpreter, "first we must eat."

"Where's the grub, we don't have any?" said Tom.

"We do," replied the Interpreter, and he touched a box which opened. He took out the contents and passed around small packages to the children. He opened his own and ate the contents.

"Is that all we get?" a disappointed Tom asked.

"You will find it is sufficient" said the Interpreter, who opened another box and took out its contents. He then turned and spoke to them; "When you have finished you may feed this to 'Smelly', but be careful, he has to trust you." He handed the food to Rachael.

After a short time, Tom said, "I don't know what that was but I feel full up."

"Hey, that must be a record, Tom's full up. What do you think of that, you two?" Charlie joked.

"Pack it in Charlie" said Mike, "where's 'Smelly', I wonder if we can get him to feed?"

Tom called out, "Come out, Smelly, it's grub up time."

Charlie joined in, "'Smelly', 'Smelly', come on, boy, we won't hurt you."

"Maybe we could put the food down and move away, then he might eat it," suggested Tom.

"Great idea," said Charlie, "see, if you really try you can make the old brain box work."

Tom ignored the jibe and put half the food on the ground at a distance he judged to match 'Smelly's' usual distance from them. 'Smelly' appeared out of a shadowy area at the base of walling. He crept over to the food, watching and tasting the air. He looked at the children, then the Interpreter and began to eat.

"Don't move anyone," said Rachael, "he's OK so don't spook him."

'Smelly' finished the food and looked up at them.

"Do you think he wants some more?" said Tom.

"He sure looks like it," said Charlie, "here, give me the grub and I'll see if I can give him some."

"I'll do it" said Tom, "I feel he trusts me."

"Oh, go on then" said Charlie.

Tom knelt down, placed the food in his open hand and gently coaxed 'Smelly' to come to him. Tom was elated to see 'Smelly' gradually crawl towards the outstretched hand.

"Easy Tom, you're doing fine, he's nearly there; well done" said Mike.

"He won't bite, will he?" asked Rachael.

"No he will not," came the voice behind them.

'Smelly' was confident now and ate from Tom's hand until all the food was gone. He remained at Tom's hand and appeared to search Tom's face; his eyes instead of roving everywhere peered directly at him. Tom responded by quietly talking to him and very, very, gently touching 'Smelley's' coat in a stroking manner. 'Smelly' permitted this intimacy and Tom found the coat harsh and coarse, however he persisted in the stroking whilst talking continuously in a level tone. 'Smelly' decided he would trust him and edged to Tom settling against his knee. Tom felt warmth from the creature and more, but didn't understand his feelings completely, he did feel 'good' and this was sufficient.

The Interpreter spoke, "Tom, you have bonded, take care of him, as I said before he will be in need of your protection."

Tom and the others didn't understand, but were too preoccupied with 'Smelly' to query the remark.

The Interpreter continued, "Tom, he will be close to you at all times, be mindful of that."

"I will" said Tom, and was happy.

Charlie turned to the Interpreter and asked, "What's in the other boxes?"

"All manner of things try one and see what happens." The Interpreter waved his hand across the array of boxes.

"I don't know, I'm not sure, it could be anything, couldn't it?" said Charlie.

The Interpreter said to them all, "Who will choose; who can overcome their fear?"

"I will," said Rachael, "what do I do, point to a box or what?"

"You touch one and I will open it for you," said the Interpreter and he moved closer to the boxes.

Rachael hesitated and said, "I don't know how to choose, they are all the same apart from the markings."

"Rely on your intuition," the Interpreter said.

"OK here goes," Rachael said, and then walked to the boxes and touched one with blue and small areas of green markings inscribed in the centre of the panel.

The Interpreter opened the box, the children did not discern the technique used, and took out what appeared to be a replica of a human eye set in a flexible mount. Rachael stepped back close to Tom who was kneeling down talking to 'Smelly'.

"Careful Rachael you nearly stepped on 'Smelly'" said Tom.

"Sorry Tom, but did you see what was in the box?"

"No I didn't, I was looking after 'Smelly', why what is it?" Tom said in a vague manner, his attention remaining on 'Smelly'.

The Interpreter interrupted, "It is not something to worry you. It is a device which lets the wearer see beneath surfaces which they ordinarily would not contemplate doing."

"You mean you wear this thing over your eye to make it work?" said Rachael.

"Excellent Rachael, that is precisely how it works, do you want to try?"

"What will I look at and what happens if I don't like it?"

"You wear it over one of your eyes as you said and close the other. If you are disturbed by what you see just open your other eye and all will be familiar to you." The Interpreter continued, "It will not show you much in here but if you go through that doorway over there you will find a multitude of things to see."

Everyone except Tom looked the way the Interpreter pointed and discovered a small doorway set in the wall beyond the boxes.

"I didn't see that door when we came in here did you?" said Mike.

"No" said Rachael and Charlie together.

"Are you going in Rachael?" asked Mike, who then spoke to the interpreter, "Can we all go in?"

"Of course you can, but only Rachael will see beneath the surfaces; and Rachael remember two things, do not remove the eye until you return here and allow me to do it and if you are at all unhappy with what you see, just open your normal eye and all will be well. Is that absolutely clear?"

"I suppose so," said Rachael.

"Go on," said Charlie, "it should be fun. Maybe we can all have a go after."

"After I'm the guinea pig you mean," said Rachael.

"We'll be together, and if you don't like it you can uncover your eye as he said," Said Mike.

"Alright, are you coming Tom?"

"No, I'll stay here and look after 'Smelly'."

"Do we have to keep calling him 'Smelly', can't we think of a better name?" said Rachael.

"I've got used to it now" said Tom, "and he responds when I use it, so I want to keep it."

"Alright" said Rachael, "but we're going in now, you sure you don't want to come?"

"Sure, see you when you get back," said Tom, and he returned his attention to his friend.

The three of them entered the area beyond, with the door closing behind them. As soon as the door was firmly shut the space before them gradually illuminated revealing a panoramic scene vaguely similar to an earth jungle. Intense green foliage was everywhere, large tree like growths reached up to a canopy of interwoven feathery branches, some hanging down others, traversing from branch to branch. Amongst all the super abundance grew colour soaked circular and elliptical 'blossoms': reds, golds and deep purples, some as small as a hand, others as massive as two metres across. The larger blooms had centres of interlocking spirals of coloured filaments with the reds, golds and purples suffusing together, producing a myriad of colours ever changing as they oscillated within the main bloom. The ground at the base of the vegetation was covered with a lemon-yellow moss-like growth which looked soft and warm, inviting bare feet to explore. The moss was divided along its length by a stream which slowly meandered parallel with the vegetation. The fluid was clear and Mike noticed something. He said, "Look there's creatures in all this jungle, including the stream, do you see them, over there and there?"

"Yes, I do" said Charlie, "there's lots of them, they're all over the place, come on Rachael you must be able to see them?"

Rachael saw movement amongst the vegetation creatures in the top, middle and lower levels; there were some on the moss, and the stream seemed to be alive with movement. They ranged from fast moving winged creatures flitting from branch to branch to slow four-legged woolly tree climbers. In between these two, creatures of varying sizes flew, leapt, crawled and ran amongst the growths. The moss attracted one specific creature and these seemed to forage on the moss, but were constantly looking around. They made no sound.

"This is something else, the more you see the more you do see. Tom should have come with us he would love it," said Charlie.

Mike agreed and said to Rachael, "Are you going to try that eye, see what happens?"

"There's no need, this is fabulous as it is."

"Yes, I know, but just try it for a minute, after all it's why we're here isn't it?" said Mike.

Charlie joined in, "Yes I forgotten about that, go on Rachael have a go."

"If I must, just to shut you two up."

Rachael carefully placed the 'eye' over her right eye. "Nothing's happening" said Rachael.

Mike reminded her: "Remember you have to close the other eye."

Rachael slowly covered her left eye with her hand.

"Well?" said Charlie "What's happening?"

"Hang on a minute; let me get used to it. Ah, it's coming into focus now, I can see in and through the foliage; oh no, no, I don't want this, I'm not looking any more, stop it, please stop it."

"What's up Rach, you OK?" Mike touched Rachael on the shoulder.

"No, I'm not, I can't stand it."

"Take your hand away, take it away."

Rachael remembered and snatched her hand away from her eye. "Thank god, that's a relief; I want to go back now."

"What did you see?" demanded Charlie.

"I don't want to talk about it; can we please go back now?"

"Yes of course," said Mike, "Come on Charlie, we're all going back now."

Charlie complained about not being ready and wanting to stay longer but Mike insisted and ushered them back through the doorway. Tom barely acknowledged their return and the Interpreter had his back to them.

"You OK Tom?" said Mike.

"Yeah sure, I'm fine, how'd it go?" Tom looked up but did not get up as 'Smelly' was on his lap apparently fast asleep. Tom took a second look and said, "Rachael, you feeling OK, you look very pale?"

"Yes, yes, I'll be alright in a minute, don't fuss."

The Interpreter turned and said to Rachael, "Perhaps you should give me the 'eye', I think you saw enough." The Interpreter gently and with extreme care, removed the 'eye' and returned it to the box, shutting the door.

"More than enough, why did you let me see all that?" Rachael replied.

"It's all there to be seen by everybody, special eye or no; most shut both eyes," he said. 'We have to move on now. Tom you have done well, keep him close to you and be prepared to hide him if necessary."

Chapter 8.

Land of Plenty.

*Realizing they had found the way; they would
achieve so much more. More and more and it
was simple. Multiply and repeat, that was the
secret.*
*They followed the creed and became
important and respected. So they carried on,
the formula worked and they were pleased.
The Lizard was quiet and no one went on the
straight road out.*

The Interpreter led them away passing through
another doorway to one side of the boxes. This
brought them to a wide pathway constructed
of finely burnished stones dressed in random
but interlocking shapes. The stones emitted
suffused hues varying from pale terra cotta to
deep magenta, which combined and seemed to
invite the walkers to proceed along its curving
route. They looked to the far distance and
made out a crenulated skyline punctuated by

domes and jagged spires. The daylight was fading, which added to the clarity of the silhouette.

"We go along this path; I want to get to that place over there just as its getting dark," said the Interpreter.

None of the group queried his instructions; Rachael was quiet and this affected all of them.

Suddenly Charlie said, "Do you realize, Tom's not said he's hungry for a long time?"

"I am but I have to look after 'Smelly'," replied Tom.

"Wow", said Charlie, "that's got to be another record, Tom not putting his belly first."

Mike was concerned for Rachael and said, "Feeling any better now; that looks an interesting place we're heading for, maybe we can get something to eat and have a rest?"

"Hope so, I need some rest. Can you stop Charlie taking the mick out of Tom, he shouldn't keep going on?"

Mike spoke to Charlie and all became quiet again.

The Interpreter stopped, turned and faced them. "We will be entering the place over there soon; it will be safe for you all except 'Smelly'. You will see many things, some will please you some will not. Tom, you will, on entering, keep 'Smelly' out of sight at all times. Do you understand?"

Tom nodded and then said, "What will hurt 'Smelly' in there, maybe its best if I stay outside?"

"No Tom you must keep with the others, there are risks if you split up and that also applies to you Charlie."

The Interpreter moved off. His manner had done nothing to lift their spirits and they continued in silence. They approached a gateway consisting of stone turrets either side of a huge door ten metres square made from planks crisscrossing and overlapping each other. This pattern arrangement revealed small triangular apertures through which they could see glimpses of light and movement. The Interpreter hesitated and then said, "Follow me, and Tom, now is the time."

Tom covered 'Smelly' beneath his jacket and they watched the Interpreter go to the gate. He walked to the right turret and spoke through a small opening in the stonework. He stood and waited. Slowly the gate eased open but only sufficient to permit them to enter in single file. Tom was last, and as soon as he was through, the gate closed.

Daylight had faded and the buildings within the boundary walls were lit from within and externally. All shadows seemed to be eliminated by the extensive lighting, creating a flat and barren landscape. The group looked around, and as their sight adjusted to the level of illumination, they discerned that the buildings were not continuous but arranged in blocks with spaces between them of about a metre. These gaps were brightly lit. The buildings themselves were of varying heights, some were so high as to be almost out of sight, and a minority at a much lower level. Walls were perforated with triangular openings through which light spilled out and was absorbed by the general level of lighting. The blocks were arranged in groups, which in turn formed greater triangular blocks. The 'streets' formed a maze-like layout, and the group were at a loss to choose a direction. Adding to their confusion was the constant throng of 'People' walking in different directions seemingly intent on urgent matters. These 'energetics' were taller than the Interpreter, thick legged and with barrel shaped bodies, and their heads were round and hairless. They had no ears, and had triangular shaped eyes which peered intensely with a fixed gaze. The head of these 'energetics' was forced to move side to side to enable the eyes to have a greater span of vision. The whole scene presented a vista of mechanical manikins walking aimlessly with head movements synchronized with leg movements.

"Stay close to me, and Tom, well done but don't relax your care. We will now find some food and a place to sleep," said the Interpreter.

"Do you hear that Tom, fo-oo-ood.?" said Charlie.

"Great," said Tom, "I must admit I could do with a good nosh."

They followed the Interpreter along the various paths and halted before a different type of building. This was long and low; in addition to the ubiquitous yellow white lighting, serried rows of coloured lights clustered together to form triangular shapes. It appeared to them to be some form of eating place as many 'People' sat at a counter eating and drinking.

"This looks good," said Tom.

"Not here," stated the Interpreter, "quickly, we must move on."

They did as they were instructed, following the Interpreter who had quickened his pace.

"Why couldn't we eat there?" said Tom.

"I'm not sure, but did you get a whiff of the food?" said Mike.

"Yes I did, it was familiar but I thought that was what's under Tom's jacket," said Charlie.

"You don't think they were eating...?" said Rachael.

"I'm not sure, but Tom wouldn't be able to tell for obvious reasons," said Mike and then continued, "It makes sense, you know, why the Interpreter hurried us past. Anyway, keep up; we don't want to lose him."

The Interpreter slowed down, reverting to his usual rhythm. Even at this pace the group had difficulty in keeping in touch, as the scurrying 'People' steered around the Interpreter, whereas they had to negotiate around the 'energetics', as they showed no intent of deviating from their chosen path. The Interpreter stopped beside a different style of building which consisted of a simple facade of doorways and window openings of rectangular shapes. This contrasted sharply with the overall triangular shape of the block in which it was embedded. The Interpreter went over to a door and pressed his hand against a panel set in the wall. The door opened and he beckoned them to follow.

They entered a large square room, the space seeming cramped by a low ceiling. The walls were plain and the floor a buff sheet material. Furnishings consisted of several wooden tables, each with upright chairs of simple design. The room was empty.

"Sit down where you will. Tom, you can let 'Smelly' out now, he is safe in here. Food and drink will be provided shortly," said the Interpreter.

Tom opened his jacket and placed 'Smelly' on the floor. Tom sat beside him. 'Smelly' stretched, shook his coat into shape and looked around. He was relaxed.

"Will he have some food?" said Tom.

"Yes, you will all be provided with suitable nourishment."

They all sat down except the Interpreter.

"So far so good. Everybody OK?" said Mike.

They were about to answer when an internal door opened and two 'People' entered carrying plates and food. The food was placed in front of the visitors with a single portion set to one side. The 'People' stroked 'Smelly'. They acknowledged their guests with a nod, but did not speak and returned through the doorway.

"Did you notice those persons, whatever you call them, had eyes that moved. The ones in the street didn't?" said Rachael.

"Can't say as I did," said Charlie, "anyway are we going to try this food or not?"

They cautiously tasted the food and found it to be delicious. Tom reckoned the separate food was for 'Smelly' and he set it down on the floor. 'Smelly' immediately sniffed and proceeded to eat, making snuffling noises of satisfaction.

"Are you not eating, please come and join us, we are happy to share?" Rachael said to the Interpreter.

"Thank you, Rachael, I will."

He sat down with them and Rachael shared out the food. They ate in silence; the food was filling and satisfying, it also seemed to quench their thirst. 'Smelly' was first to finish, closely followed by Tom.

The Interpreter holding up his hand said, "We must sleep now. Tom don't worry about 'Smelly' in this place, he will follow you, but when we go out tomorrow you must be vigilant again."

He then got up and waved them to follow. He went through a doorway at the far end of the room into a corridor. The doorways led off at intervals, the Interpreter then said, "You may choose any room to sleep and you will find washing facilities and such. We will be away early in the morning and I will awake you."

"Which room are you having?" said Tom.

"I don't sleep. Go ahead and rest," replied the Interpreter.

They checked the rooms which were all similar in size and layout and they each chose a room. Mike's room was square in proportion again with a low ceiling. The walls were muted plain colours and relieved of anonymity with some form of paintings, using vivid colour combinations forming swirling patterns; delineations of colours were curved and extravagant as if the artist had broken free of rigidity and luxuriated in time and space. Everyone prepared for bed and tried to sleep.

In the morning they were awoken by tapping on the doors; sleep had overcome the disquiet of their surroundings. They washed and dressed and assembled in the corridor. The Interpreter stood at the far end adjacent door.

"Follow me; we must be on our way."

The group moved towards him when Rachael stopped and said, "Hold on a minute, we haven't said 'thank you' for the food and rest. How do we do it?"

"I have made sure your gratitude was expressed, now please follow me," replied the Interpreter.

As they approached a door at the end of the corridor, they heard and felt a tremendous explosion which sounded at the entrance area they had previously used. The Interpreter immediately held up his hand and instructed them to be absolutely quiet. Charlie started to question the Interpreter but was instantly cut off by him and received such a stern look that he subsided into reluctant silence. The Interpreter put his finger to his lips and pointed towards the nearest room. He ushered them into the room and softly spoke, "We are in great danger, please do not speak, you must remain here until I come back for you." As he was speaking they could hear muffled sounds of explosions and sharper more penetrating sounds. He continued, "The welcoming people who gave us food and shelter are not liked by the majority of outsiders: the ones you saw between the buildings. They must have seen us enter this building and are using it as an excuse for attacking our hosts. Although they, our hosts, have done no wrong, the outsiders resent them giving hospitality to strangers. And remember you are strange to them. Now they will attempt to break down the outer walls to expose the interior and reveal your presence. You must be vigilant, stay away from the outside wall and if you think it is going to be breached, move to an opposite room but stay clear of the outside wall."

Mike began to speak, but again the Interpreter stopped him before he could utter a sound and said, "Do not for whatever reason, speak or make a sound, your lives may depend on it. I will go now and help our friends. Remember, any sound you make will be heard outside, they cannot hear me as long as I speak quietly."

The Interpreter walked out of the room leaving the group to look at one another. Mike held up his hand in a gesture of 'be quiet', and moved over to the inner wall encouraging the others to follow. Sounds of explosions continued but seemed a distance away. They leant against the wall in a close group, as if finding security in its solidity and each other. A tremendous roar assailed their ear drums and the outer wall shook and partially collapsed at high level. Rachael grabbed Charlie and Tom and rushed into the opposite room, closely followed by Mike. Tom dropped to his knees scrabbling around for 'Smelly'. The animal had followed Tom and nudged him in the leg. Tom choked off a cry of relief and cuddled 'Smelly' against his chest. They leaned against the inner wall and looked at each other, faces pale and drawn. Dust swirled in the air and more explosions continued jarring their nerves. The Interpreter appeared through the dust again, with his hand held high for silence. He leaned down and whispered: "We must go soon, please remain silent or you will be discovered. When I signal, follow me quietly and take extra care not to make any noise walking through the debris."

He stood up and remained stock still for what seemed to them like many agonizing minutes, until they collectively felt their situation was hopeless. Eventually the Interpreter signalled they should follow him. He moved out into the corridor, now littered with smashed walling; doors and beds lay haphazardly, forming obstructions to their progress. Dust filled the air. He picked his way towards a door set in the end of the corridor. Twice he abruptly stopped and held up his hand. They all stopped and listened intently. They could make out spasmodic noises of explosions and sharp cracking noises, but these were at the far end of the building, away from them. Slowly the Interpreter edged to the door and checked for any sounds of movement outside.

Holding his hand up again he motioned them to follow, but extended a finger to indicate they had to wait. He also indicated by signs that they should make no sound when outside. All of them nodded their comprehension as they negotiated obstacles, desperately trying not to create any sounds. Finally, he eased the door open and moved forward, with the children following. Outside the noise of the attack assailed their ears and they looked to the Interpreter. He looked around, and satisfied of their safety, slowly moved away from the building. He led them along streets formed by the familiar triangulated buildings and they followed the Interpreter avoiding 'energetics'. Gradually, the buildings became less congested, more spaced out and lower in height. The noise from the attack diminished and they began to feel slightly more relaxed.

They came to a clear area, which stretched for about two hundred metres, bounded on one side by massive masonry walling twenty metres high and buttressed by inclined square blocks at ten metre intervals.

"Can we speak now?" said Charlie.

Rachael motioned Charlie to be quiet, then the Interpreter said, "It is alright to speak but Charlie, you should have waited for my signal. Please think a little before you act." He continued, "We should be safe now, but we must move on."

"What will happen to the people who gave us food, will they be OK?" asked Mike.

"They will, they have a secret way out of their building in emergencies, but I am sorry to say they will be unable to return to their home. They will have to find somewhere else to live until they can make a new one," replied the Interpreter.

"I don't understand why they were attacked, was it just because of us?" said Rachael.

The Interpreter thought for a moment and said, "You were the excuse for the hostilities, the real reason is much deeper rooted."

Charlie and Tom became distracted by the colossal structure in front of them.

"Look at that, that's some castle, I wonder who lives in there. Can we go in?"

The interpreter stopped and said, "Charlie, do not always assume. Behind those walls is what you would call a lizard."

"I like lizards," interrupted Tom.

The Interpreter continued, "This lizard is a giant, which is why those walls are so huge. Before the construction of them the lizard (who was smaller then, but still large) used to invade the town and take 'People' to eat. The people managed to provide the lizard with other food long enough to build the ramparts. Now the lizard is so huge it is lazy and listless. When it is hungry it eats part of its tail. Enough, now we have to travel round the walls and continue our journey. Tom be very careful. This way."

Charlie was disappointed and mumbled about not having any fun. He lagged behind until Rachael shouted at him to keep up.

They cleared the extremity of the walling and walked along a rough track, devoid of bends or changes of direction. To one side was open land, barren and free of vegetation and trees. Bordering the other side were rows of low buildings, row upon row, stretching into the far distance. Each building was uniform: brown in colour with a flat roof and approximately three metres wide and twenty metres long. The buildings were spaced three metres apart end to end and side to side. Set into the sides were slots or narrow openings caked around their edges with brown dusty accretions. Roofs were penetrated with funnel shaped flues from which emanated a grey brown haze. As they passed alongside these buildings a breeze wafted over them.

Rachael cried out, "That smell, it's the same as 'Smelly' only ten times worse."

"Yes, it is, I reckon that's coming from those buildings over there," agreed Mike.

"That means they're full of..." said Rachael, as she choked off the end of the sentence.

"It will take a long time to pass this area, I suggest we hurry on," said the Interpreter.

All of them increased their pace until they cleared the buildings.

"Can we have a rest now, I'm knackered?" said Tom.

"Not yet Tom, we have to be totally clear of this area before it's safe to let 'Smelly' out."

Chapter 9.

Simple.

Confess they demanded. So we responded:
"We made a mistake, but don't worry we'll
find a way to put it right."
And they did. The cost they ignored; what
else could they do?

The Interpreter slowed his pace and said to Tom, "'Smelly' will be safe now, you can put him down."

Tom uncovered 'Smelly' and gently placed him on the ground. 'Smelly' did his usual shaking to rearrange his coat, and then looked up at Tom.

The Interpreter stopped and spoke to them: "We will now visit a totally different place and I ask you to be respectful." He turned and walked along a grassed pathway, they followed somewhat puzzled by his remark.

"We're off again. I wish I could have seen that lizard," said Charlie.

"Only if you wanted to be its dinner!" said Mike.

Rachael butted in; "This way you lot, look there's some buildings or something over there."

"Not more towns, I've had enough for now, can't we just sit down and have a rest?" asked Charlie.

"We may get some rest soon, perhaps when we are in the town or whatever it is," replied Rachael.

As they neared the town 'Smelly' ran ahead and Tom shouted, "Hey 'Smelly', don't run off."

Tom started to run after him.

"Don't worry Tom, he is quite safe and will find you later, he will not be lost," said the Interpreter.

Reluctantly Tom ceased chasing 'Smelly' and re-joined the party, but was glad of the chance to regain his breath. As they drew closer to the buildings they could make out a variety of shapes and materials. Entering the town, there was no boundary walling or gateways. They gravitated to the Interpreter who had stopped. He turned to speak to them.

"You may go anywhere you wish, even split up, visit many places, talk to everybody (they will understand you and vice versa) and enjoy the experience."

Rachael was about to speak, but the Interpreter held up his hand and said; "We will all meet by that tall building over there which will be lit up on the outside as it gets dark. It will be the only externally lit building and you will be able to see it from anywhere provided you remain within the area of the buildings."

Charlie and Tom made to wander off, but then Rachael said, "Don't go too far you two, always keep the tower in site, and stay together."

"We will," said Charlie, "don't worry about us, he said its OK"

"What about 'Smelly', he's disappeared?" said Tom.

The Interpreter reassured Tom: "He will come to no harm, Tom, and will return to you later." He then turned and disappeared amongst the buildings.

Tom and Charlie set off and Mike said to Rachael, "Let's explore together. From the Interpreter's description it sounds a friendly place, what do you reckon?"

"Yes, OK and if Charlie or Tom don't turn up we can agree what to do."

"Sure, but they'll be fine. Come on let's go."

They looked around and up at the tower. Despite its height it seemed welcoming, with surfaces making mosaic patterns. Many openings and doors showed the interior at low level, upper levels also had many openings, each one complete with a balcony. 'People' sat or stood on the balconies, and as Rachael and Mike looked up they looked down on the strangers and waved.

Rachael said to Mike, "They really are friendly, do you think we should wave back?"

"Can't do any harm; yes, let's give them a wave."

They both waved, and more waves were returned.

"Now what do we do, it seems rude to just walk away?" said Mike.

Before they made a decision a 'People' emerged from the tower and said, "Would you like to come in, you are welcome?"

Mike hesitated and then decided, "Yes please, we would like that."

Rachael looked at Mike, but followed him into the tower's interior.

They entered a large circular space with a domed ceiling high above them. The floor consisted of uneven buff coloured flagstones, and the walls were covered with woven hangings of various cloths and designs. The domed ceiling was a soft blue which shimmered from the light entering through the doors and openings. The whole effect of the room was a kaleidoscope of colour, always providing interest and warmth to the onlooker. There were many 'People' in the room, some standing, some sitting at bench tables. They were similar in stature and build to Mike and Rachael. They wore robes of a smooth material, ranging from yellows to reds and greens. Females, if that's what they were, wore lighter robes of a looser material and of a more flowing design with brighter hues of the general colour schemes. The 'People's' faces showed large eyes set wide apart, a vestige of a nose and a wide mouth which seemed to smile often but showed no teeth. Abundant hair covered their head, falling onto their shoulders. The whole effect to the onlookers was a mixture of fear and wonder.

Rachael remembered the Interpreter's words and whispered to Mike, "Don't forget we have to be respectful."

"Yes of course," replied Mike.

The 'People' who had invited them in gestured with his arm and said, "Please come in and sit down, we have food to refresh you if you wish."

"Thank you we would be grateful for your hospitality," replied Rachael.

"Good," said the 'People', "Mike and Rachael would you like to sit over there?"

Mike stuttered out some words, cleared his throat and asked, "How do you know our names?"

The response came as a shock to Mike and Rachael; "The Interpreter, as you know him, explained the situation to us, he's a good friend of ours."

"But he hasn't been in here, he went away in another direction," queried Mike.

"Of course, I'm sorry I did not explain. He doesn't have to be with us to communicate; we can be in contact over quite a distance. Now, let me arrange your food."

Several of the 'People' went out to an adjoining room and returned with food, but no drink. The food was ladled from a large wooden bowl into smaller bowls of similar shape and wooden spoons were set to one side. Many of the 'People' joined Mike and Rachael, one said, "Please try the food, we hope you find it to your liking."

They began to eat and Mike said to Rachael, "This tastes really great, it melts in your mouth, you don't have to chew it."

Rachael responded enthusiastically, "Yes it does and it quenches my thirst."

They all finished the food and a 'People' said, "We hope you enjoyed your meal and it was sufficient."

"Yes, thank you, we were very hungry. What is the food made from, it's really delicious?"

"It is from local plants we grow, harvest and mix in various amounts to produce different flavours. You have just tried our favourite, we call it Silame. We're pleased you found it appetizing."

"We certainly did," said Mike, "it was and also seems to act as a drink. Thank you we appreciate your kindness."

"You are welcome, it's not often we have fresh company. Would you like to view our place from the tower top or explore the areas on foot?"

Mike looked at Rachael and said, "Could be good, you up for it?"

"Very funny, yes let's go, sounds interesting."

A 'People' said: "Follow me; we will go using the water lift."

The three exited the room and stepped onto an open platform.

The 'People' then said, "Hold on to the side rails as the movement can get jerky sometimes depending on the water rate. Shouldn't be too bad, we haven't had much rain lately."

He pulled a lever and the platform slowly moved upwards, gradually gathering some speed. The platform jerked occasionally and the 'People' flexed his knees to compensate for the uneven motion. Mike and Rachael tested letting go of the railing but quickly regained a hold as the platform wobbled.

"Not long now, you are doing fine," said the 'People' as they slowed and came to a gentle stop. The 'People' then said, "we have arrived, have a good look around. When you wish to go down just stand on the platform and push this lever, not forgetting to hold on, it will take you all the way and automatically stop at the bottom."

He walked away from them and entered a room off the platform area.

"That was good, let's have a look round," said Mike.

"Sure", said Rachael, "this way looks as there's a viewing balcony outside, come on."

They went out to the balcony, which traversed around the tower providing a panoramic view of the buildings far below. The view presented a vista of individual dwellings of varying shapes and sizes, none standing out as being much larger than the majority; some were quite small as viewed from the balcony, and these were attached to a larger building by pathways lined with shrubby growths. The general layout of dwellings appeared haphazard, no overall plan could be discerned but there was space around every building; pathways wandered sinuously between and around them seemingly without obvious purpose. 'People' could be seen walking in groups to various dwellings or just standing in groups and presumably talking.

One area caught the attention of Rachael who said, "Look, down there," and she pointed to a gathering in an open area in which 'People' were milling around, "see them, they certainly seem intent on what's happening. Shall we go down and have a look?"

"Yes, back to the platform for a ride of your life, this way, roll up, roll up, it's free so don't hesitate, your captain will be the one and only Mike the man. Come on Rach it wasn't that bad coming up."

"Mike, my name is…"

"OK, OK, sorry. Can we go now?"

They walked onto the platform and Mike said, "This is your captain speaking, please hold on the railings, the weather is fine and the water supply is excellent. Here we go."

He pushed the lever and they began to descend, slowly at first then gathering speed until Rachael began to be concerned as the bumps and judders became more pronounced.

"This is great, I wonder if it goes any faster?" said Mike.

Before Rachael could respond, the platform slowed and the bumps reduced in intensity and frequency. They came to a gentle stop and a 'People' greeted them, "Did you enjoy your visit?"

"We did, thank you" said Rachael, "and can you tell us what was happening somewhere over there, there was a lot of going on?" And she pointed in the direction she thought was correct.

"Of course, it's the day of games (for us); they would be playing 'Souble' as we call it. Please go and watch, you will be welcome. Just follow the path from this doorway, stay on it and you will hear the noise," he laughed and continued "you won't get lost, goodbye."

Mike and Rachael took to the path which meandered between and around dwellings until they began to doubt they were heading in the right direction.

"Shush, I want to hear for sounds if I can," said Rachael.

They stopped and listened intently. Suddenly a cheering noise broke the silence.

"Yes, that's it," said Rachael, "it's coming from over there."

The direction of the sound was contrary to the direction of the path, so they stood, uncertain whether to proceed or retrace their steps.

"He did say stay on the path, we'll go a bit further and see if the sounds get louder," said Mike.

"Yes captain Mike, whatever you order!"

"Sorry to be bossy, but someone has to take charge of this expedition!"

"Is that what it is, then lead on 'Oh Intrepid One'?"

They continued, sometimes hearing the sound distinctly, sometimes faintly. More cheering was heard, louder and more distinct, so they decided to remain on the path. Their confidence grew as they neared the sounds which were now virtually continuous. Following a sharp bend, they arrived at an open space filled with 'People' all congregating around a roughly rectangular space about ten metres long by six metres wide. There was no discernible barrier around this area but the 'People' stayed clear of it as if by mutual consent. Within the area six 'People' stood at one end chatting, at the far end to them a vertical post was set in the ground. This was about one metre high and positioned about two metres from the end of the 'pitch'. Attached to the post, and facing the players, were three shiny discs each about five centimetres in diameter. The top disc was a glittering blue, the central a bright green and the bottom a dull red. A gong like sound vibrated through the air and Mike and Rachael attempted to view the proceedings by looking between the 'People' spectators, but they could see parts of the whole area. A 'People' turned and spoke to them; "We have visitors, welcome, please pass through here and go to the front, you will have a much better view."

"Thank you, but we cannot push in," said Rachael.

"Please, you are our guests, we are happy to see you and you will not offend us at all," said the 'People'.

Rachael and Mike expressed their gratitude and followed the 'People' through the crowd which eased apart as they passed through to the front area. The six 'People' separated into two groups, and all of them looked at the two visitors and waved. Mike and Rachael confidently returned the gesture. The gong sounded again, higher pitched than before. One team stood away, the other moved forward to a line marked on the ground. The first of the team held a bright cyan coloured ball which fitted into his palm. He was right handed and swung his arm backwards, and then accelerating a forward movement released the ball towards the post. The ball bounced twice and struck the red disc, making a metallic cymbal sound. The spectators cheered and the competitor stood down. The ball remained adjacent to the post. The second player repeated the throwing action, only this time with a white ball. Again the ball bounced twice but failed to hit a disc, the ball remaining where it had finally landed. The spectators issued a breathy sigh. The third player stood at the line and released a golden ball which bounced once and struck the blue disc. The disc emitted a singing sound, oscillating in watery musical vibrations. Mike and Rachael felt the sound stimulating and at the same time relaxing. The spectators were silent. The first team retrieved the balls and then stood back to allow the second team to move into place. The three players each threw their ball; the final player making a two-bounce strike on the blue disc. A gorgeous sound sang out and was partly obscured by shouts of pleasure from the spectators.

Rachael asked Mike, "Why are they cheering now, but didn't when the first one hit the blue disc?"

"I think you have to bounce the ball twice before it hits the target," said Mike.

"Oh; strange game. No one is jumping about celebrating the winner. Good atmosphere though," said Rachael.

"Do you want to see another game, looks like more teams are coming on the pitch, or shall we explore some more?" said Mike.

Rachael looked around and said, "Hang on a minute, we're supposed to be able to see the tower, yes there it is. Great, yes let's go, you can follow me this time."

Rachael marched away from the games area and continued along the original path. They relaxed and enjoyed the walk, occasionally meeting a 'People' who smiled and waved as they passed.

"You know, of all the places we've seen, this is, how can I describe it, I am at ease, comfortable or such, do you know what I mean?" said Rachael.

"Yes, I feel the same, its great here; sometimes I forget we're not at home and all that, although that does come and go from time to time," said Mike.

"Sometimes I totally forget this is all unreal and we're in the hands of the Interpreter, but what can we do, we must look out for each other. I wonder what Tom and Charlie are up to?" said Rachael.

"I know, let's see if we can find them and at the same time see anything else of interest, what you reckon?" said Mike.

Meanwhile, Tom and Charlie wandered along the network of pathways, not concerning themselves with direction or location of the tower.

"Come on Tom, let's see what's over there." said Charlie.

Tom agreed and they went over to a small compound surrounded by a low fence. Within the fencing there was about ten to twelve 'Smelly's' who were chasing and racing each other. One broke away and ran over to Tom.

"Hello 'Smelly'," said Tom, bending down to stroke his friend.

Other 'Smelly's' came over to investigate, and for the first time, Tom and Charlie heard them utter soft nasal sounds. Tom's 'Smelly' jumped around and around and suddenly completed a somersault. Others joined in until the mass of small bodies filled the area with movement and sounds.

"No doubt about it Tom, you sure connect with these creatures, I almost forgot the smell, not quite though!" said Charlie.

"But what are they doing here; they could easily jump over the fence?" said Tom.

Charlie shrugged his shoulders and said, "Don't ask me, they are happy here by the look of things."

A 'People' approached and said, "Hello, I observed your interest in these you call 'Smelly's', they are here to, let's see, what you would call, socialize, I think. They are free to come and go as they please. The fence is only to delineate their area so we and perhaps visitors such as yourselves do not intrude. I see one of them is attached to you Tom; he will return to you later, do not worry."

"How do you know Tom's name and you mentioned other visitors, are there any here now?" asked Charlie.

"The Interpreter informed us of your presence and no, we only have one set of visitors at a time, and then not very often," said the 'People'.

Charlie persisted: "How do you decide when and who comes here?"

"We don't, that is solely the judgement of the Interpreter."

Again Charlie insisted, "But he never tells us anything, so how do we find out?"

The 'People' smiled and said, "I think it is for you to find out, not the Interpreter."

Charlie became exasperated, "Find out what?"

The 'People' raised a hand and said, "Perhaps I have said too much, all I can offer you is to follow your path. Now I must leave you. Remember, return to the tower when it is lit, goodbye."

He turned and disappeared from view along a winding path.

Charlie turned to Tom and said, "You never get a straight answer around here."

"Don't worry Charlie, come on there's more to see and it's not dark yet."

Charlie shook off a sulk and said, "Come on then, which way shall we go?"

Rachael and Mike wandered the pathways, occasionally talking to 'People', sometimes stopping to inspect the dwellings.

"Did you notice we have gathered a following?" said Mike.

"I know I presume they are children as they much shorter than the ones we've talked to. Shall we see if they want to talk or play or something?"

Mike looked at Rachael, nodded and turned around to face the entourage. The 'People Children' stopped, hesitated and then laughed and chuckled amongst themselves.

"We seem to be a source of amusement to them," said Mike.

"Glad we make them happy."

One of the 'Children' stood at the forefront of the group and said, "We are not laughing at you, we are just happy to see new visitors, please don't be upset."

"Of course not, can I ask you your name?" said Rachael.

"We do not have names; we know each other by sight and at a distance. Do you have names?"

"Yes, my name is Rachael and this is Mike."

"We are pleased to see you Rachael and Mike. Is there anywhere you want to go; we can show you the way."

"We don't know what there is to see, can you suggest something?" said Rachael.

"There are many things, perhaps you would like to visit our gardens we look after?"

"Yes please," said Rachael.

Mike whispered to Rachael, "Now who is being bossy!" Louder he said, "Thanks we would like that."

"Follow me, this way," said the 'Children Spokesman'.

Rachael and Mike followed the leader and became surrounded by the others who gently touched their clothes, eventually taking it in turns to hold the hands of Mike and Rachael. They rounded a bend in the path and viewed a magnificent vista. Plants of varying heights filled the area, showing reds, blues, greens, to yellows, oranges and mauves. There was no formal layout, no apparent plan or organization. It all presented a matrix of colour and shapes.

"Do you like our garden?" said the 'Children Spokesperson'.

"It's magnificent, beautiful; I've never seen anything like it," said Rachael.

Mike agreed adding his praises.

"What do you do about weeds?" said Rachael.

The 'Children' looked at one another then back to Rachael. The 'Spokesman' said, "We do not know that word, can you explain?"

"Oh, you mean the word, weeds."

The 'Children' nodded.

"Well they are plants that we don't want in our gardens, ones that spread everywhere or are not attractive."

"I see," said the 'Children', "we do have plants which perhaps are not as striking as others, but we look after them all. Please have a closer look and you will see."

Rachael and Mike edged closer to the garden boarder. "Look Mike, yes there are more plants than I thought. Some quite plain, some just leaves; the more I look the more I can spot."

"You're right Rachael. I wonder if they have insects, bees and so on, to pollinate the flowers?"

Rachael thought for a moment and said, "We could ask, but they didn't understand the word, weed, maybe it's too difficult."

"Let's give it a try, can't do any harm."

Rachael again turned to the 'Children' and asked the question: "Do you have insects that fly into the flowers to produce more?"

The 'Spokesperson's' face lost its open demeanour and the others became still. An intangible quiet pervaded the area and after a long pause the 'Spokesperson' said, "We made a mistake a long time ago. We now do the work of the flying creatures, by hand, ourselves. We miss them."

Mike said to Rachael, "I think we should go now, shall we move on?"

Rachael agreed, "We'd better I suppose."

They said their thanks to the 'Children' and waved goodbye. The 'Children' became animated again and returned the waves.

"It's beginning to get dark, see the tower is showing its lights, time to head back and meet the others," said Rachael.

They walked on along the twisting path confident it would lead them to the tower.

Tom and Charlie continued their exploration and found many interesting events to watch; games requiring dexterity or physical skills and precision judgements. None of them held Charlie's attention for long and he dragged Tom away in search of greater excitement. Tom reluctantly followed.

He eventually said, "Charlie, it's getting dark, it's time we went back to the tower."

"You go if you want; I'm carrying on to find something a bit more entertaining."

"We ought to stick together, come on, we should go back," said Tom.

An irritated Charlie then said, "Go on then, if you think you won't get lost, I can find my own way."

Tom unsure, paced back and forth until Charlie said, "You trying to wear out the ground?"

Tom had had enough and said, "OK, I'm going."

Tom left and made his way back to the tower. On arrival he was greeted by Rachael and Mike. The Interpreter nodded to him.

"Where's Charlie, I thought you two were together?" asked Rachael.

"He went off on his own, so I came back on my own."

As they were discussing what to do 'Smelly' arrived and went up to Tom.

"Hello, I wonder where you've been, good to see you," said Tom.

'Smelly' performed a quick somersault and then sat at Tom's feet. Tom bent down and picked him up and they both enjoyed the reunion.

"It's good 'Smelly' came back to you but we have to find Charlie; where did you leave him, Tom can you remember?" said Rachael.

Tom prepared to reply but 'Smelly' wriggled in his arms to get down.

"Hold on, 'Smelly', I'll drop you, stop struggling."

The Interpreter spoke to Tom, "Trust him, let him down."

Tom lowered 'Smelly' down to the ground and looked at the Interpreter. 'Smelly' ran a few metres away and then returned halfway. He repeated this action, gradually moving further away.

Tom again looked at the Interpreter who said, "Go ahead Tom."

"Got it!" said Tom and hurried after 'Smelly' until they were out of sight.

"Will they find Charlie?" said Mike.

"'Smelly' will, they will return soon," said the Interpreter.

"Sometimes Charlie just doesn't think; why does he never consider other people?" said Rachael.

"He follows his head; he's a bit impetuous, that's all," said Mike.

Rachael was about to reiterate her worries when Charlie, Tom and 'Smelly' appeared. Mike placed a hand on Rachael's shoulder without effect.

"Charlie! We've been worried about you, where have you been?" said Rachael.

"Just looking around, why what's the panic?"

Mike stepped in; "No panic, Charlie, we were concerned, we thought you and Tom were together, that's all."

"He decided to run back here, I wanted to see some more, is that a crime?"

The Interpreter spoke, "Charlie, learn, be aware. Now it's time to go."

"But it's dark," said Rachael.

"It is, we would have made a good start but for the delay. Please follow me."

The Interpreter turned and led them away from the tower, branching off the pathway into semi-darkness.

Chapter 10.

Invasion.

Rallying as one they congregated, lined up in
formation and were correct and willing.
Reinforced by shape and colour
They moved as one.
Energy moving to collide with energy. The
wasteland was complete.
For the onlookers there was hope.

The Interpreter, Rachael, Mike, Tom with
'Smelly', and Charlie bringing up the rear,
continued walking along a narrow path.
Looking back, the children saw the tower in
the distance.

"I really enjoyed being in that place, I
wonder why we have to move on," said
Rachael.

"Please pay attention, this is extremely
important, we have to pass through a potentially
dangerous area, attend to my instructions at all

times, there will be no opportunity for error," said the Interpreter.

"Did we ever have a choice?" said Charlie.

"You always have a choice, Charlie. Make sure you take the necessary responsibility for it."

Charlie was somewhat chastened by this remark and for a change was silent.

"This way and be alert," said the Interpreter.

He moved on, followed by the children, who became somewhat subdued and worried about the possibility of impending danger.

Mike then said to Rachael, "We need to be serious about this, we should keep an eye on Charlie, not let him drift away."

Rachael agreed.

The path led to an extensive plain, bordered on three sides by tree like growths, similar to the ones near the Right Hooker's City but without the internal illumination. The plain was flat, lifeless and covered with scrub grasses flattened into a dull grey matted texture. In the far distance, just discernible, was a gap in the trees.

"We need to reach that opening on the edge," said the Interpreter and pointed, "through there and we will be safe from this area of conflict."

Charlie moved as if to start crossing the plain.

The Interpreter said sharply, "Not that way, we must go around the edge against the trees over to our right."

Charlie sighed, "But that's the long way around, it's much quicker if we go straight across."

"Not if we get caught up in the assembling of the One Eyes Army. Now follow me and if there should be reason I will direct you to enter the trees but only as far as the shadows hide you from the plain."

Charlie persisted, "Why can't we go into the trees now and be safe?"

The Interpreter said quietly, "It will slow us down and deeper in the woods will be some Right Hookers looking for stray One Eyes. Now we go."

The Interpreter led them alongside the wood edge at a swift pace, quite unlike his usual steady rate. The opening they had targeted seemed a great distance away. Rachael manoeuvred herself behind Charlie and Mike brought up the rear.

At an instant the Interpreter sidestepped into the wood and ordered, "Quickly, into the shadows."

All of them edged into the trees.

The Interpreter urged them into the shadow area and said, "Stay still and be quiet, there will be plenty to watch, but do not reveal yourself."

They wondered what was to happen, but did not break the requested silence. Charlie's compliance with this may have been due to Mike's hand on his shoulder.

Emerging from the woods opposite there appeared to be members of the One Eyes Army. Scores of them began filling the plain. At first there was no discernible pattern, just a confusion of One Eyes milling around. As if by some unspoken command they formed into groups of twelve, each group forming into a diamond shape, orientated to point towards the city of the Right Hookers. The diamond shapes spread out equidistant from each other and aligned with respect to one another. The effect was to present individual diamond shapes grouped to form larger diamonds; the whole forming one giant diamond. Charlie was about to whisper to Tom when the One

Eyes stood stock still in formation and silence fell over the army. A single One Eye soldier walked through the centre of the diamond from end to end, stopping at the head facing the opposing city with his back to the army. He wore a loose shawl over his shoulders, the back of which displayed a large black diamond shape enclosing a red circle in the centre. He held a single staff which carried a banner marked with the diamond and circle motif. The soldiers also wore shawls with the same insignia, but the circles were black. The leader made no speech and merely raised his staff.

Charlie edged beyond the trees.

Mike whispered, "Charlie, get back, you will be spotted."

Charlie merely waved a hand in annoyance and muttered, "I'm behind these shrubs; they can't see me."

Rachael moved to pull Charlie back, but the Interpreter restrained her saying, "Too late, stay here in the trees, there's nothing we can do."

The leader of the army turned slowly and pointed his staff, firstly at Charlie's location and then to the diamond formation closest to

Charlie. This formation, as one, rotated ninety degrees and slowly moved towards him.

The Interpreter spoke quietly to Charlie, "Charlie, just stand still, do nothing and say nothing. We all depend on you to obey my instruction, none of us will be safe if you panic or speak." The Interpreter then told the others to remain absolutely still and not to speak or make any sound whatsoever.

The diamond formation approached Charlie and he could see the individuals in more detail. They were uniform in height and build, and their faces were long and narrow with black eyes set deep in protruding foreheads, appearing to float within their cloaks. The cloaks were grey green and seemed to be of a semi-stiff material, and as far as he could see, concealed hands, if indeed they had such appendages. The leader of the diamond led them to Charlie.

The Interpreter, in a barely audible whisper, said, "Hold on, Charlie, hold on."

The diamond moved forward, slowly and deliberately until the leader stopped just short of Charlie. Charlie was transfixed by the appearance of the silent and impassive inquisitor, and became rigid and unable to move or speak. The diamond leader continued moving and stopped a few millimetres from Charlie. Charlie couldn't look away, and as if hypnotized, stared into the eyes opposite him. The eyes betrayed no life; there was no colour, as if life had been extinguished and replaced with automated responses to fixed stimulus. Charlie became aware of a tingling in his head and was about to shake his head to rid him of the sensation when he remembered the Interpreter's previous words of warning. Rachael gripped Mike's hand so tightly he almost rebuked her, but he also remembered the Interpreter's instructions. Tom stared at Charlie wishing the diamond would go away and they would be safe. The Interpreter stood still and viewed the confrontation of Charlie and the Diamond inquisitors intently.

Silence descended around all of them and the sense of time to them felt suspended, as if the events they were a part of had ceased to have movement: there was nothing but an interminable silence. The standoff, if that was what was happening, persisted with no resolution. The tension felt by Mike, Rachael and Tom became unbearable, but the Interpreter's words of warning returned to their minds, unspoken, but heard nonetheless. Charlie remained still unable to move in spite of his instinct of flight.

The tingling in his head ceased and the leading diamond 'person' raised an arm, or some part of his body unseen, as the cloak moved to continue concealment of the body. The raised cloak became stationary, remaining in this position with no indication of further action. Rachael and Mike became concerned as they both thought the raised cloak might be a request for reinforcements. Tom vowed to himself that if Charlie did become in danger, he would dash out and drag him into the safety of the trees. Charlie remained static and frightened at this new development. The leader of the army again raised his staff, pointed at the out of formation diamond and then rigidly to the front. The diamond moved slowly towards Charlie and the front 'person' quickly stepped around him, followed by the two outliers moving to either side of their captive, effectively enclosing Charlie within the diamond formation. The Interpreter, with great strength and concentration, silently communicated with all the children, urging them to be still and silent. All obeyed, including Charlie, who by now was rigid with fear and a sense of helplessness. All obeyed, that is, except Tom, who, in spite of his bulk, dashed across towards Charlie, and ducking beneath the cloaks, joined him within the triangle. Smelly did not follow him. The Interpreter continued his exhausting connections with Mike and Rachael.

Tom whispered to Charlie, "Charlie, come on, we can get out under the cloaks, come on before they do something."

Charlie looked at Tom and as if coming out of a trance said, "OK, ready?"

Tom nodded his agreement and they both made to escape, but were halted as cloaks were lowered to block any exit. For reasons they didn't understand both Charlie and Tom were reluctant to touch a cloak. They both felt a tingling in their heads and felt weak and without energy.

The tingling continued and they felt compelled to turn around towards the leader of the army. The leader raised his staff, pointed to the out of formation diamond and then to the ground in front of him. Slowly the instructed diamond, complete with captives, moved towards the leader, finally stopping at the indicated position. Charlie and Tom had offered no resistance, shuffling along within their prison. They looked up at the leader who was taller than the diamond soldiers, but of similar appearance in all other respects. He leant slightly towards the captives and the tingling in their heads now permeated throughout their whole bodies, making them slightly nauseous. He continued staring at them, showing no emotion and remaining perfectly still. Although Charlie and Tom were both terrified and felt the intensity of the leader's lifeless eyes, they both wished something would happen. They had lost the sense of time, but the feeling of everything around them was in a state of immense pressure; all was absolutely still and they felt any slight movement or sound would precipitate some terrible action, something beyond their control and out of reach of those hidden in the trees: even the Interpreter remained hidden and appeared unwilling to help them.

Tom and Charlie, with great effort, managed to reach out and grasp each other's hand. Immediately the tingling disappeared and they felt light and energized. Looking up at the leader they saw him raise his staff, point to them and then towards where they had first become prisoners. Immediately the enclosing diamond retraced their original journey with Charlie and Tom remaining within the diamond and stopping in their correct formation position. The end soldier moved to one side allowing Charlie and Tom to exit the enclosure and enter the woods. The end soldier returned to his correct position completing the diamond shape which adjusted position to complete the original formation.

The leader of the formation turned about, raised his staff and slowly moved forward. All of the diamonds, as one, moved off following their leader and maintaining their shapes with great precision. The matted grass muffled the footfalls and the ensemble moved forward, virtually silently. The Interpreter held up his hand with an open palm facing the children, keeping it in place until the last of the army disappeared out of view.

The Interpreter slowly sank to the ground and clasped his hands around his lowered head.

Rachael questioned the Interpreter, "Are you alright, what's happening?"

Looking up at the group he said, "I am exhausted, that took a great deal from me, wait a little while and I will recover."

Mike turned to Tom and Charlie and said, "Are you two OK?"

"Yes, I think so, still a bit shook up but I reckon we're OK, aren't we Charlie?" answered Tom.

Charlie nodded but did not speak.

The Interpreter got up and said, "I am not sure what happened out there to you, Charlie and Tom, I was concentrating all my effort on preventing Rachael and Mike from intervening which would have been catastrophic. But you fools seem to have escaped unhurt and so we can go now, do not delay."

They trekked along the wood's edge, the Interpreter insisting they did not risk the more direct route across the plain. Eventually they approached the opening in the trees.

Mike said to the Interpreter, "What were the One Eyes going to do, I didn't see any weapons?"

"They will collect their stash of weapons, previously stockpiled and camouflaged near the city."

"Why do they want to keep fighting, what's it about?" said Rachael.

"Let me answer by asking you a question. What do you all do if you have a disagreement amongst yourselves? I assume you do not kill each other?" Before they could answer he said, "No, please do not explain. Explain to yourselves and then understand."

Mike, puzzled, decided to change the conversation and said, "What is the other side of the opening and where does it lead?"

"All being well it will lead you to a place where you can return home," replied the Interpreter.

Chapter 11.

No Entry.

Once, they had created part of the world and
were sorry.
So they put up barriers and gave out warning
signs
and they forgot. Memory faded until the
world absorbed life and was cruel.
The past sat there solid but obscured by aged
dust.
Carelessness permitted the unforgivable.
What if?

The Interpreter's use of the word 'home'
resulted in the children stopping on the spot
and looking at one another. Rachael was first
to speak, "Do you mean we can go home,
when, how, please tell us?"

"You will see, first we have to proceed
along this way," said the Interpreter.

He moved on and all four chattered to each
other. Spirits rose and they eagerly followed

the bearer of great news with 'Smelly' close behind.

The path from the opening in the trees led away from the plain. On the left side lay open scrubland; ragged bushes grew amongst dry looking rough grasses. The ground appeared moribund and covered in a layer of dust. To the right a high bank edged the path. A mesh fence surmounted the bank composed of some sort of metal material topped by jagged sections of the netting. The banking and netting were also dust covered, as was some form of lighting fixed to the netting at intervals. Dust covered notices could be discerned at intervals but the lettering was illegible for the most part.

"What's in there, looks a bit spooky?" said Charlie.

"It does not concern you, follow on we have a distance to travel," said the Interpreter.

They walked on buoyed up by thoughts of home. Mike and Rachael discussed how they could possibly explain to their parents what had happened. Tom was absorbed with 'Smelly' who ran along and around his feet. Tom was worried lest he trod on his friend, but 'Smelly' was very agile and seemed to delight in only moving from under Tom's feet at the last possible moment. The Interpreter pushed on, maintaining a steady pace. Rachael and Mike continued their discussions. Tom was happy. The equanimity of the group became disturbed by a muffled wailing sound. The boundary lights began to flash, showing dimly through the dust covering.

The Interpreter immediately halted, turned around and viewed the children. He raised both arms and clenched his fists.

"I should not have…' he said. But his words were cut off by the sudden arrival of several 'People' dressed in white all-in-one clothes, including hoods and gloves.

"Where's Charlie, Tom, we thought he was with you?" said Rachael.

"No, he wandered back behind me, he'll catch us up in a minute," said Tom.

"I'm afraid he won't," said the Interpreter, "he has been very foolish and I cannot save him."

"What do you mean, has it anything to do with that awful sound and the lights?" said Mike.

"Yes, it means Charlie has probably entered into the area behind the fencing. No one is permitted entry, it is supremely dangerous; these 'People' you see rushing around will check the security of the perimeter, but will not enter, this area has been unused for a very long time."

"But what about Charlie, we can't just leave him in there if that's where he is?" cried out Rachael.

"There's nothing you can do, anyone going in there will perish."

Mike in desperation shouted, "We can try, we must, we must."

Tom joined in, "I'll go in. 'Smelly' can stay outside."

The Interpreter sat down, placed his head in his hands and said, "I have failed you, I haven't fully recovered, my thoughts wandered at the wrong time. It is my fault but I cannot put it right. There is no way now."

"I'm not leaving without Charlie, I'm not," said Rachael, and she sat down, head cradled in her arms.

Mike sat beside her. He looked at the Interpreter and said, "Is there really nothing to be done, there must be a way?"

"Mike, I cannot make it different, it is a disaster, but I cannot change it."

Rachael spat out words of recrimination, "You mean you won't do anything, not that you can't."

The Interpreter rose and stood looking into the far distance and said, "Your judgement of my lapse is correct, but I cannot help him no matter what you think. If I attempt to enter the forbidden area, the 'People' will prevent me."

"How did Charlie enter the area, surely it's secure?" said Mike.

"It should have been. As I said, it hasn't been in use for a long time, everyone knows to keep away."

Rachael snapped back, "Charlie didn't."

The Interpreter seemed to shrink in size and sink into himself. He looked at them and said, "Whatever I say will not ease your hurt or make things as they were, I cannot do so. I suggest we have a moment of silence to think of Charlie."

"You can't mean he's dead already, what happened to him, did he suffer. Could he have escaped before the alarm went?" Rachael begged for answers.

The Interpreter turned slowly to face Rachael and said, "Once inside that area, he was lost, the effect of the poison would have been almost instantaneous, his suffering would have been momentary."

They all withdrew into themselves and then simultaneously Rachael, Mike and Tom, put their arms around each other and began to cry.

The emotions were interrupted by a 'People' arriving and addressing the Interpreter, "We found a breach, an old access gate had corroded and someone forced it open enough to permit access; who would do such a thing, we cannot get them out?"

'I am aware, our friend is the victim and we have to move on," said the Interpreter.

Rachael stood up and shouted at the 'People', demanding to see the place Charlie had broken in.

The 'People' looked at the Interpreter who briefly nodded. The 'People, turned and walked away followed by Rachael, Mike and Tom. They arrived at the position of the forced entry. The 'People' stood to one side and the children made out a large gateway. This old entry was now sealed across with metal bars and was defended by a row of 'People.' There was no way of looking closer as the 'People' closed ranks if they moved towards them.

"We have to move on, you can do nothing here," said the Interpreter.

"Why do we have to move on, can't we stay here, I can't bear to leave without Charlie?" said Mike.

The Interpreter replied, his voice sounding flat and empty, "I have to take you to the place where you can choose to go home if you wish, but there is limited time in which to achieve this."

"How can we trust you after this?" retorted Rachael.

The Interpreter looked at the three devastated children and coldly and firmly said, "Time is short, shall we go?"

Mike turned to Rachael and Tom and said, "Do we have any choice, what can we do?"

Rachael was silent and Tom said, "I'm not leaving without saying good bye to Charlie."

"But we can't" said Rachael.

"We can," said Tom, "we can make a memorial stone or something, anything."

Mike looked at Rachael and she nodded.

"OK, let's look around for some stone or wood so we can make a tablet," said Mike.

They looked for any indication of suitable material, finding none. Whilst they searched, 'Smelly' began digging in the bank side.

Tom ceased searching and went over to 'Smelly'. He stood up and shouted, "'Smelly's' found some stuff, quick, give us a hand."

They all crowded around 'Smelly' and took over the excavations.

"Look at this, this will do," exclaimed Tom, as he pulled out a flat piece of stone.

"Well done, Tom," said Mike. "And 'Smelly', he showed us where to look."

Working together the three pulled the stone up the bank, resting it near the top. The Interpreter watched their exertions and decided to speak.

"I'm sorry to remind you, but time is short. Be speedy with your efforts."

"I will fetch a smaller stone where we got this slab; we may be able to scratch the surface," said Rachael.

Rachael returned with two hand sized stones both with some pointed edges.

"What shall we say, what do you think?" said Mike.

They discussed various wordings but none seemed to capture the spirit of loss. The Interpreter broke into their thoughts and said, "You may accept my idea as fitting your need."

CHARLIE
Lost to us and forever in our thoughts.
R. M. T.

They looked at one another and nodded.

Tom began marking the stone setting out the areas for wording. "Is that OK, I've just outlined where the words could go?"

"Yes, that's fine Tom," said Mike, "Is that OK with you Rachael?"

Rachael nodded, holding back tears as she looked at the stone.

Tom continued his inscriptions, finishing he said, "That's as best as I could do, is it alright?"

Mike and Rachael agreed it was fine.

The Interpreter interrupted their thoughts, "Please say your farewells, if you want the chance to return home we have to move quickly."

"I suppose we must follow him, seems the only way to get home" said Mike.

Tears filled his eyes as he thought of Charlie.

Mike took Rachael's hand and gently said, "I think its best if we go. Come on Tom we will all stay together," and he reluctantly moved on following the Interpreter as he turned and walked slowly along the path.

Mike held out his other hand to Tom and the three trudged behind the Interpreter. 'Smelly' followed. They continued in silence, the barren landscape and high banked fencing adding to the desolation of thought and spirit.

Chapter 12.

Going Home.

Now they retraced their steps and found the start place.
All was the same and different.
Change had been wrought, and was forever.

They moved on in silence, in stark contrast to their previous animated optimism. The surroundings changed, barren landscape and dust giving away to green foliage, bushes, trees and soft grass. The air cooled and a fresh breeze revived their spirits until memory flooded back.

Rachael turned to Mike and said, "I feel so guilty about leaving without Charlie."

"So do I," said Mike.

"It doesn't feel real, does it?" said Tom.

They agreed.

The Interpreter stopped and said in a monotone, "Shortly you will recognize where you are. I have to make sure the timing is correct, so please when I say, follow me, be sure you to stay close."

The trio said nothing and just nodded.

Continuing along a ridge with a deep valley to their left they came to a rocky outcrop.

"Rest here now, it won't be long. I will be away for a little while, please stay where you are," said the Interpreter. He walked around the outcrop and out of view.

"Are we really going home?" said Tom.

"That's what he said, so I suppose we are," said Mike.

"You don't suppose he is fetching Charlie, do you?" said Rachael.

After a pause Mike said, "I don't think so, he was certain he couldn't do anything."

"I suppose you're right, it doesn't seem right without him," sighed Rachael.

"You don't think Charlie will be at home waiting for us, do you?" said Tom.

"I'd like to think so, but somehow I think not," said Mike.

The Interpreter returned and said, "Good, the time is near. Follow me."

They, not knowing whether to be excited or apprehensive, followed the Interpreter around the rocks and into an opening leading into a dark cavern.

As their eyes adjusted to the gloom Mike said, "Wait a minute, this looks like the place we started at, when we met the Interpreter."

"You are correct, Mike, and now you all face making a decision. If you look carefully over there", he pointed to a vertical area of rock opposite them, "you will notice the light is beginning to increase. It will continue to do so and when it is at its brightest you will decide to pass through or stay here."

The children looked at one another in silence.

Mike said to the Interpreter, "What's on the other side of the light, will we be home?"

"You will return to your picnic, if you choose to stay here it will be permanent, there will be no return. Please tell me of your decision before the light commences to dim."

They hesitated, looked at one another, nodded to each other and Rachael said, "We want to go home. We are sure."

"Good, I wish you well," said the Interpreter. He took out an envelope and offered it to them, and said, "Take this."

Mike took the envelope and asked, "What's it for, do we open it now?"

"No, open it and follow the instructions when you are in your reality, not now."

Suddenly Tom spoke up, "What about 'Smelly', can he come with me?"

"I'm afraid not, Tom," said the Interpreter, a softness returning to his voice, "he belongs here, he would not survive in your reality, I will care for him and take him back to the Simple City."

Tom sat down and 'Smelly' crept over to him. Tom stroked him and said, "Sorry, mate, we have to part. I'll be sad but I will always remember you."

'Smelly' brushed against Tom's leg and then slowly wandered over to the Interpreter.

"Time. Please go to the light and when I say 'go', walk into the light. You will be safe."

They eased over to the light, which seemed to warm them even though there was no discernible heat.

"Go."

They moved forward holding hands. Instantly they found themselves at their picnic spot. The trappings of the picnic remained.

A voice shook them out of their daze, "Where have you been, we've been here since six o' clock, but you were nowhere to be found. We and Tom's parents have been searching the woods, and now suddenly, you appear. Have you been hiding from us, trying to be funny? What's going on, we've been very worried and where's Charlie?"

Silence followed the inquisition. A deep enduring silence. Mike held the envelope and wished for the Interpreter to appear to explain everything, knowing he would not.